Son of a Beard

Lani Lynn Vale

Dedication

This part is always hard for me to write. So I'm going to go with what I feel for right now.

Today is my dad's birthday. I forgot. It feels weird to think that I forgot, when ten years ago, or even five, I would've called him and or gone to visit him. It had never even occurred to me that today was his birthday until my husband mentioned it over dinner.

So, this book is going to be dedicated to him…or at least the memory of him. Of the dad that I used to have. I loved that man, and I wish that I had him back.

Acknowledgements

Kellie Montgomery—one of the most amazing people, and editors I know. Thank you for taking my babies and making them perfect.

Asli—Thank you so much for loving my books as much as I do. They need you like I do.

Danielle Palumbo—I don't even think I can call you an editor. At this point, you're like a lifeline. You're the woman that catches my plot holes and tells me when shit doesn't jive. Thank you for everything that you do.

Furiousfotog/Golden Czermak—Don't ever stop taking photos. They're pure gold.

Tank Joey—I love your beard, and it fit this book and character perfectly.

Mom—you deserve just as much recognition as anyone does. Thank you for spending your days off with my babies—both literally and figuratively. You're the best damn dad (and mom) ever.

CONTENTS

Other titles by Lani Lynn Vale:
The Freebirds

Boomtown

Highway Don't Care

Another One Bites the Dust

Last Day of My Life

Texas Tornado

I Don't Dance

The Heroes of The Dixie Wardens MC

Lights To My Siren

Halligan To My Axe

Kevlar To My Vest

Keys To My Cuffs

Life To My Flight

Charge To My Line

Counter To My Intelligence

Right To My Wrong

Code 11- KPD SWAT

Center Mass

Double Tap

Bang Switch

Execution Style

Charlie Foxtrot

Kill Shot

Coup De Grace

The Uncertain Saints

Whiskey Neat

Jack & Coke

Vodka On The Rocks

Bad Apple

Dirty Mother

Rusty Nail

The Kilgore Fire Series

Shock Advised

Flash Point

Oxygen Deprived

Controlled Burn

Put Out

I Like Big Dragons Series

I Like Big Dragons and I Cannot Lie

Dragons Need Love, Too

Oh, My Dragon

Dixie Warden Rejects

Beard Mode

Fear the Beard

Son of a Beard

I'm Only Here for the Beard

The Beard Made Me Do It

Beard Up

PROLOGUE

*I don't understand your specific brand of crazy,
but I do commend your devotion to it.*

-Truth to his ex

Truth

"Anybody home?" I called loudly as I came out of my workshop.

Destiny didn't answer and I frowned.

I could've sworn I heard something.

"Destiny?" I rumbled, peaking my head around the corner of the bedroom of the single bedroom shotgun house I shared with her.

Empty. As was the bathroom that I could see due to the door being wide open, and all the lights being on.

I could see Destiny's makeup, clothes, and shoes strewn all over the floor of not just the bathroom, but the bedroom as well.

She'd gotten dressed in a hurry.

Normally, she didn't leave the expensive dresses I'd bought her lying in a heap like that unless it was because I'd thrown it there after ripping it from her body.

And boy did she have a sexy body.

That was the only thing keeping us together at this point. The sex—or the sex we used to have. We hadn't had it in a while, and at this point, there wasn't much keeping us together.

It was always good, which made it hard to kick her to the curb because she was convenient.

If I didn't have her to come home to, I wouldn't have the nightly sex I craved.

And I wasn't the type to spread my dick around to the women that I knew I could land. They always had expectations.

Destiny, however, did not. She didn't expect me to marry her. Hell, a lot of nights she didn't even expect me to come home at all.

Which was good seeing as I was a member of The Dixie Wardens MC, Mooresville, Alabama chapter.

Sometimes I spend the night at the clubhouse after a club party—which she most certainly did not go to—and she doesn't complain.

Growling when I saw the empty bracelet box that was supposed to contain the bracelet I'd bought her for Christmas, one she wasn't supposed to wear unless it was a special occasion due to the fact that it cost several thousand dollars, was laying haphazardly on the night stand. I turned off the light and headed to the front door.

The kitchen was empty, as was the living room as I passed through it on my way.

So what had I heard?

Something caught my attention before I could get there, though.

Some motion.

I could see something moving outside through the sheer white curtains that Destiny insisted we had to have, and I stopped, my eyes narrowed as I focused.

That was where I parked my bike.

On the side of the house, hugged right up against the window so I could see it as we passed in and out of the living room.

That bike was my baby.

The absolute best thing that'd ever happened to me in my entire life.

And someone was sitting on it.

Was it Destiny?

I hated when she did that.

She'd lean on it when she went outside to talk on her phone, because I'll be the first to admit that she was obnoxiously loud when she was on the phone, and I would complain if she didn't go outside.

I'd tell her not to lean on it, because her weight could offset the balance of the kickstand and cause it to smash into the side of the house, and then I'd have to fix a dent or a scratch, and I most assuredly didn't want to do that, but she'd do it anyway.

Just to piss me off, I was sure.

So that was what I expected as I flicked open the curtains to peer outside.

I'd been about to raise my finger to tap on the glass when what I was seeing through the window finally registered in my brain.

Destiny was on my bike all right, but some man was on it, too.

Some man with his balls laying unbound against the leather of my seat.

The leather that I'd fucking stitched by goddamned hand.

The leather that I'd searched high and low for and specifically chosen after finding it in a motherfucking magazine.

The leather that'd seen no one's ass but mine—and not even that was bare.

Anger welled up inside of me, and I finally took my eyes off the man's balls sticking to my seat going up to the man's face, and that's about when everything exploded.

Because it wasn't bad enough that they were fucking on my bike.

No, the man that Destiny was fucking on my bike was my cousin.

The same cousin who made my younger years a living hell with his teasing about my pretty boy looks and my "girlie" hands.

Hands that were now rough and strong from years of doing what I loved—being a swordsmith.

Somehow, I found my Colt .45 in my hand, and somehow, I pointed it at the man's head.

And before you get all bent out of shape, the safety was on.

He, however, did not know that.

Tapping on the glass with the gun, I made sure that the laser in the grips was activated and pointed right at about eye level.

So when he turned toward the sound of my tapping, he got a red laser straight to the eye, causing him to look up and blink at me in confusion.

I let up off the laser, allowing him to see just what was waiting for him, causing him to freeze.

"Get off my bike," I growled.

The window muffled the words, I was sure, but he got the gist of what I said fairly fast.

Hopping off and dislodging his pee-wee sized cock from Destiny's pussy, I watched dispassionately as she fell to the ground in a wet pile of dirt, causing her to cry out in confusion.

She looked up in bewilderment at Kenneth, my asshole cousin, who was busy trying to tuck his tiny pecker back into his perfectly tailored slacks, and followed his gaze.

I let my real feelings out from behind the veil I was using to contain them with, and Destiny understood completely.

She was boned.

Well and truly boned.

***

Verity

Two days later

I was excited.

This was my last dress fitting before the big day in two weeks.

Which would be the day that I married the man I loved, Kenneth Lee Reacher. I would be Mrs. Kenneth Reacher, and I thought that had a mighty nice ring to it.

Giddy beyond belief, I took a hold of Randi's hand, my best friend in the whole wide world, and started marching with purpose to the front door of the best dress shop in Mooresville, also known as my Good Grandma's place.

"GG!" I cried as I opened the door.

I was confronted with my grandma's most annoying employee, Tiffany, and instantly I wilted.

"Is my GG here, Tiffany?" I asked as nicely as I was able.

"No. Mrs. Cassidy is out of the office until tomorrow afternoon. What can I help you with?" Tiffany asked sweetly.

I narrowed my eyes.

My grandma wouldn't be out of the office unless this witch of a woman hadn't told her that I was coming. Which I most certainly relayed to Tiffany this morning on the phone when I'd called.

Fucking bitch.

"I'm here to try my wedding dress on," I murmured.

Tiffany's eyes moved down my body with barely disguised disdain, and I had to tighten my hand on Randi's hand to keep her from moving forward and pummeling her fist into Tiffany's face.

It wouldn't do to lay a beat down on my GG's longest standing employee, even if she was a bitch.

She was a hard worker, and she was good at her job, something in which my GG informed me of each and every time I made mention of how shitty she was.

"Okay," Tiffany's smile was weird.

Like she was trying to hide something.

Something that I wasn't going to like.

A weird feeling started to filter into my thoughts, and I worried that there was something wrong with my dress…like she'd intentionally altered it too small so I wouldn't fit into it.

And that would be embarrassing, because I already had enough trouble with my weight. I didn't need that extra worry of having to get my dress altered again two weeks before my wedding.

"Right this way," Tiffany waved her arm.

I glared at her back, and her tight little black dress that was painted onto her like a second skin.

She looked good in it, but I couldn't figure out why she dressed so provocatively. She was supposed to be making brides more comfortable on one of the most important days of their lives—not making them feel inferior by showing them up with what she was wearing.

But that was just me.

Maybe other ladies didn't have the same problem that I did.

"She's such a bitch," Randi grumbled under her breath. "Do you think your grandmother would hate me if I tripped her and made her break her face?"

I squeezed Randi's hand.

"Don't."

Tiffany pushed into the room where I'd been fitted for the last six months, and I came to a dead halt when I saw my dress.

On another woman's body.

"What. The. Fuck," Randi screeched.

Most people didn't understand Randi's and my relationship.

They thought we were lesbians, which couldn't be further from the truth.

We were best friends and had been since we were in pre-K.

We shared everything together, something that Kenneth hated.

He despised sharing me with Randi, and I guess that should've been my first indication that Kenneth wasn't all that he was cracked up to be.

But I kept kicking things under the rug and hiding them when I should've been letting them out of the dark and bringing them into the light.

Because if I had, I might've realized sooner that things weren't as good as I thought they were.

That there were things going on that were having an adverse effect on our relationship.

But I didn't, and that's why the next five minutes went over like a truck crashing into a small economy car.

I sat there, motionless, as I watched the blonde woman turn around, my dress on her body, a perfect fit, as she looked at me with a secret smile on her face.

"What the heck is going on?" I asked Tiffany.

Tiffany's face was the picture of innocence. "I was informed by Kenneth two days ago that this dress was to be fitted to Destiny's liking. Is that wrong?"

Is that wrong?

"What?" I asked, confusion clouding my features.

I couldn't think straight.

Why would Kenneth care about another woman's body fitting into my wedding dress? Unless that dress wasn't actually my dress at all, but a nearly exact replica.

It looked to be about four sizes smaller than the one that I'd had.

Surely that wasn't my dress.

Surely.

"That's not my dress, is it?" I asked, relief flooding through me. "But why would Kenneth care what she wears?"

I didn't even know her.

How did Kenneth know her?

Speaking of the devil, my phone rang, and I pulled my phone up to my ear and answered immediately.

"Kenneth," I said. "I'm trying to get my dress fitted, and some lady is here wearing a dress that looks like mine that they say you ordered it for her to wear and to have fitted to her liking."

"Shit," Kenneth cursed. "V, we need to talk."

I hated when he called me V, but that wasn't something I could control. He did it whether I asked him to stop or not, so what was the point in correcting him?

I should've corrected him, because the next twenty minutes were spent with him explaining in that condescending tone of his that 'you're so damaged, V,' and by the time he was finished, the only thing I wanted to do was to completely obliterate the letter V from the English language.

Oh, that and change my name of course.

CHAPTER 1

Let's settle this argument like adults...in the bed...naked.

-Truth to Verity

Truth

"One man's used up slut is another man's brand new bride."

I can see now that that wasn't the best way to start my best man speech.

Then again, I was still trying to figure out why the hell Kenneth asked me to be his best man in the first place. Especially since the bride he had just married had been my girlfriend just a few short weeks ago.

But whatever.

For some reason, he'd asked me, and my own morbid curiosity had me saying yes. Why, exactly, I'd agreed was still yet to be determined, but I probably should've at least considered not drinking before I came to this shitstorm farce of a wedding.

Outraged gasps filled the air around me, but I didn't take my eyes off of the bride and groom, who were staring at me venomously as I grinned back at them.

What had they honestly expected me to do?

I was a biker. I was also known to be the kind of man who spoke his mind.

I hadn't been happy about the fact that my woman had fucked some other man while being in a relationship with me. I haven't always been happy with her, though, she would've still been with me had I not witnessed that.

It'd been right at three weeks since I'd caught them fucking on my bike.

Yes, let me repeat that.

I caught them fucking. *On. My. Bike.* I have to keep saying that in my head because I still can't believe I saw it.

My bike meant the world to me, and I hadn't been able to sit on it without thinking about them since then.

Motherfuckers.

A snicker from my side had me turning to see the girl that I'd walked in with tonight.

The same girl who looked like she wanted to be here about as much as I did…which wasn't much at all.

I was now regretting my position as best man, and if my mother wasn't here to witness me abandoning my duties, I might have left already.

That girl, though… the brunette with the wavy hair in the dress that was painted onto an ass to die for? Well, she almost made it worth it.

Almost.

The only thing that would turn my frown upside down was a goddamned beer. So it figured that the one wedding in the history of all weddings that needed alcohol the most didn't have it.

IE, this one.

"I think it's time to give up the microphone, T," I heard said from my side.

I turned to find my cousin, Eugene, looking at me with a thin sheen of sweat dotting his brow.

"What?" I asked. "You wanted to give a best man speech?"

I was an asshole.

My cousin, Eugene, had a fear of crowds.

For him to even attempt to get the microphone away from me took balls on his part, but I was one pissed off man, so I wasn't giving him the mic, even though he did ask nicely.

"N-no," he shook his head adamantly. "I was t-trying to…"

He stopped speaking when I held up my hand. "Then let me finish."

He sighed and backed away, turning his apologetic eyes to his brother, Kenneth, and then went back to his seat.

Kenneth punched him in the arm the moment he sat down, and I wanted to punch him in the face.

Little fucker.

He needed to go fuck himself.

It wasn't his brother's job to do the dirty work, and I wasn't stopping until I either got an apology or was kicked out.

And lucky for everyone here watching the show, he would never offer me an apology.

Because offering an apology would be admitting that he'd fucked up, and Kenneth Lee Reacher didn't admit when he was wrong.

Which was always his downfall.

And me, Truth Alan Reacher, well, I was going to make sure he saw the error in his ways.

CHAPTER 2

Sadly, I'm all out of damns. However, if you're interested in a flying fuck, I have a few.

-Verity's secret thoughts

Verity

I didn't want to be here.

In fact, I wanted to be here about as much as I wanted to have my left nipple placed in a nipple clamp and twisted right the hell off.

But nobody asked me what I thought.

Nobody cared that I didn't want to be a witness at the wedding I was currently attending.

The wedding that I'd painstakingly planned, and then was told two weeks ago that I was no longer needed as the bride, because, you know, brides are apparently interchangeable.

Oh, but my mother had kept the account, because she was a businesswoman after all.

Money was money, honey.

The sound of my mother's annoying voice made my hands clench.

Then the man started talking, and the breath left my body.

Not because he took my breath away, but because he said what I was thinking.

"Fucking slut."

My eyes snapped up and over, and it was then I saw the man that I'd walked in beside two hours before.

No one at this entire wedding looked like they wanted to be here less than me. Except that man. He looked like wanted to be here nearly as much as I did, which was not at all.

This tall, dark, and dangerous man with his brown hair buzzed clear down to his scalp, and those stunningly bright green eyes that looked like they could see straight down to my soul.

Then there was the scruffy beard framing straight white teeth, not to mention his tattoos.

An entire sleeve of tattoos extended down his left arm, starting at some point I couldn't see beneath his black t-shirt, and trailing all the way down to his wrist where his big ass Luminox watch rested. A watch that I knew cost a whack because I'd bought my father the same one last year for Christmas.

He also wore it wrong, too. Like my dad. He had the watch face on the inside of his wrist, so all he would have to do to check the time was turn his palm to face him and he'd be able to see it perfectly.

According to my father, it took a whole lot less effort to check the time.

Not that I'd ever disagree with him, but at the time I'd thought he was weird.

Now, seeing it on this man, I realized that maybe it did take less effort.

"Ummm," I finally tore my eyes away from his mouth. "What?"

The muscles in his arms flexed as he turned only his head to face me…yeah, those muscles were just icing on the cake.

"I said, 'Fucking Slut,'" he repeated. "The bride. She's a fucking slut."

I blinked, then I nodded in understanding. "Why yes, yes she is."

I would know. I'd walked in on her husband to be, now my ex fiancé, and her fucking on my bed. On my family quilt. Next to my goddamned cat. After the dress fitting from hell. And after he told me the engagement was over, but apparently I needed a visual.

The man's mouth twitched, and I had the weirdest urge to run my fingers through his magnificent beard.

"What's your name?" he asked, breaking into my thoughts.

"Verity," I answered immediately. "What's yours?"

He smiled.

"Truth."

"My name means Truth," I informed him.

"I know," he answered. "That's why I smiled."

"Two peas in a pod," I shrugged.

He snorted. "So…did he cheat on you?"

He gestured toward the groom, who was busy feeding his new wife a piece of the cake that I'd picked out.

"Yes," I replied just as bluntly as he'd posed the question. "In fact, that's my wedding cake that they're eating. Oh, and that wedding dress? Also mine."

He turned sharply to stare at me, trying to figure out if I was being serious or not.

"Then why the fuck are you here?" he asked.

I sighed.

"I don't want to talk about it."

Not now. Not when I could potentially break down and cry in front of that asshole.

He didn't deserve to see my tears.

"How about I take you for a ride on my bike, and we find somewhere to fuck?"

My mouth dropped open.

"And then you can tell me what that asshole did to you, and I'll share what the slut did to me."

I nearly choked on the air I inhaled, if such a thing were even possible.

"Uhhh," I hesitated. "Okay?"

I wasn't normally so slutty, but hell, if you saw this man, you'd have jumped at the chance to do him, too!

He grinned, showing off those perfectly white teeth again and I nearly moaned.

"All right, who's ready to hear the speeches?" my mother called excitedly over the intercom.

That was said over the loud speakers at the front of the room, and I knew it was a good time to leave.

"Ready now?"

Did he sound hopeful?

I nodded sharply, and then stood and offered him my hand.

He stood too, took my hand, and started to lead me outside.

But then someone stopped him before we could make it to freedom.

Shelley, Kenneth's sister, had her hand on his arm.

"Don't you want to give your speech?" Shelley batted her eyes at Truth.

The words weren't said maliciously, but I knew they were meant to hurt, all the same.

"Oh, yeah," Truth snapped his fingers like he'd completely forgot. "I guess I'd better do that right quick, now shouldn't I?"

Shelley's eyes widened, and she reached for his hand, but he was already gone, heading straight to the DJ booth that I'd also had a part in picking out.

"Give me the microphone," he snapped at the DJ.

The DJ, not a stupid man by any means, nodded mutely and held it out to him.

"Thanks," he muttered, before turning to face the room.

I moved to put the wall at my back, allowing me to see both Truth and my ex fiancé and his new wife, all the while waiting to see what the man I'd just met was about to do.

I knew it would be good…I just didn't have any idea *how* good.

"How's everyone doing tonight?" he asked into the mic.

The crowd around the new happy couple all turned to stare at Truth, and I pressed my lips together.

"Where do you think you're going, young lady?" my mother hissed. "You have to stay here for the remainder of the night, or you're not getting paid."

I gritted my teeth and turned to my mother, hoping that my fury at her for forcing me to attend didn't show on my face.

"I was only obligated to stay an hour, per your contract," I told her. "Nothing else was ever said about me doing anything past my obligation."

"You will not get paid. I swear it. If you leave, all that money is mine."

All the money wasn't hers.

All the money was both of ours.

I was the silent partner that helped fund my mother's business when she started to go under. I was the one to bust my ass day in and day out to make sure that everything was perfect for this wedding.

And I was also the one that had been here only out of obligation.

So no, I knew my legal rights. I owned fifty-one percent of the company. I didn't have to do a goddamn thing, and I'd still make money.

Why? Because that'd been the stipulation when my mom had come to me about this business opportunity in the first place. I offer the money and the business sense, and she does all the legwork.

Even though I'd done the majority of the legwork for this particular wedding.

See, I had a trust fund, and my mother did not.

Why? Because my mother had already blown through hers.

However, when I'd turned twenty-one and my great-grandmother had died, leaving me over two million dollars, I'd invested my money like a smart girl who had a money hungry mother to show her everything not to do.

And in the seven years it'd been invested, I now had over six million dollars.

Not that I dressed or acted like it.

In fact, I still had my job as a customer service representative for the Mooresville newspaper.

Why? Because I couldn't quit.

Literally, each and every time I tried to find the courage to quit, my mother would pull a stunt and I'd use work as an excuse.

It was a vicious cycle. And, one day, I would be able to get out of the dead-end job and do my passion, which was blowing glass, for a living. I would be able to do it all day long, and take long naps in the middle of the afternoon.

But until I finally found the courage to stick up to my mother, I was stuck.

Well and truly stuck.

Like right now, for instance.

I wanted to leave.

The man had literally taken me by the hand, and here I was standing next to my mother listening to her bad mouth me.

"One man's used up slut is another man's brand new bride."

My mouth dropped open as those words came from that sexy mouth I'd been admiring all night, and I did the worst possible thing that I could do at that moment.

Giggle.

"Verity," my mother hissed. "Don't you dare."

I narrowed my eyes.

"Leave me alone," I growled under my breath. "I can laugh if I want to."

"Not when they're paying a half a million dollars for this wedding, and I'm the one that'll get the bad review if this goes south."

My gut clenched. "You spent how much?"

Her mouth thinned. "You heard me."

"You don't still have my credit cards, do you?" I gasped, worry etching my face.

She closed her mouth and shrugged.

"If I find one single cent of mine paying for this wedding, I will ruin you," I crowded her. "I have no loyalty to you. I have absolutely none. Trust me. You burned every single bridge that would ever make you a mother to me, so I will lose not a single second of sleep turning you into the police for fraud, and filing a freakin' lawsuit against you if I have to…and I'll leave you a negative review on Facebook."

She gasped, "You wouldn't."

Seriously? Out of all the things I'd said, it was the negative review on Facebook that caused her to gasp in outrage?

"All right, ladies and gentlemen. I'd just like you all to remember that you should definitely watch your wives and husbands around these two. They're a fine pair, and they don't care if you're family or not. Nobody's relationship is safe around them."

Those words sounded in my ears, but I didn't take my eyes off of my mother as she stared at me in scorn.

"I didn't use your credit cards, but you should probably call and cancel them, because I know for a fact that you still have everything stored in your joint account on Amazon, where a lot of it came from." She crossed her arms over her chest. "Though, I had nothing to do with that. The bride provided it all for me, and said her 'fiancé' gave her free reign with his account."

My mouth thinned. "I'll take care of that."

And boy, would I.

I was going to go to the police department tomorrow and file charges against the woman.

And if I could sneak in any other charges while I was at it, I'd do that, too.

"So, in conclusion, I would like you all to know that I have a motorcycle for sale. The seat's gone, but the rest of it is in perfectly working order," the man I was about to leave with, said.

I found my second smile of the night.

I'd heard the story while I was listening to my mother, but I didn't expect him to sell his motorcycle.

I presumed he was going to just replace the seat.

Obviously not.

***

Truth

Twelve hours later

Vegas wasn't a good idea.

I wasn't really sure how we ended up here, either.

I think it was actually the airline's fault.

I mean, honestly, why the hell did they offer flights to Vegas at all hours of the night?

And why the fuck did they sell tickets to drunk people? Because that was what Verity and I were…drunk as skunks.

We were in Vegas now and drinking even more.

Apparently, it wasn't illegal to have open containers while walking down the strip in Vegas...or if it was, none of the cops stopped us.

Then again, I'd seen quite a few other things that were clearly more pressing than two individuals with open containers.

Such as the man riding his unicycle naked, yelling something about how everyone was going to die since tonight was the end of the world.

Then there was the old lady with her tits tucked into her pants running around with a 'Kill all extraterrestrials' flag.

That one had been more traumatizing than any war I'd ever seen.

I could deal with blood, guts and gore, no problem. I apparently could not handle an overweight elderly woman with her nipples poking out where her vagina should be, though.

"There!" the woman at my side demanded, smacking me on the arm.

I turned to survey the chapel that she wanted to enter.

"That's a chapel," I told her. "Why do you want to go there?"

"Because I just saw two motorcycles pull in, and I want to know why."

And that was how, in a completely unplanned, surprise turn of events, we got married by a couple of bikers.

I was still dressed exactly in what I'd been wearing at the previous wedding I'd attended. A pair of faded blue jeans that I used to work in, a black t-shirt, biker boots, and my cut.

The woman at my side, however, had changed.

Into a strapless number made purely of leather, that did fucking amazing things for her already banging body.

Full, perky tits spilled out of the top of the dress.

It hugged the curves of her rounded hips before coming to a stop at the top of her tanned thighs.

Yeah, I wasn't completely blaming the alcohol for the reason I married her.

I would, however, blame the way she was completely murdering that dress with how she filled it.

I didn't normally go for a full-figured woman.

But this woman, my God was she stunning.

She was absolutely, drop-dead gorgeous, and I let my dick do the thinking.

Just like the way I let my dick do the thinking two hours later as we finally made it into our hotel room.

I did, however, manage to cover my cock in a condom before I sank completely inside of her.

And it continued to do the thinking as I fucked her mercilessly. On her back. On her knees. On our sides.

Then she got on top, and I lost all ability to think.

We'd never actually managed to get her dress off of her before I was inside of her.

What we did manage to do, though, was get her panties off, and her breasts above the top of her dress.

And when she was riding me, her breasts were bouncing this way and that.

Her long, thick brown hair was waving about us every which way.

And God, did her pussy feel like heaven.

Something I told her over and over again as I professed my undying devotion to her beautiful cunt.

And hours later, when dawn finally started to kiss the sky, we fell into a breathless heap on the bed, and slipped into an exhausted sleep.

The next afternoon when we finally woke up, the reality of the situation hit us, and we somehow came to a decision to ignore everything and sweep it under the rug.

Which we thought would be easy since neither of us remembered much from the night before.

Looking at our naked, entangled bodies, we thought that was all it was.

Oh, how wrong we were.

CHAPTER 3

I already want to take a nap tomorrow.

-Verity's secret thoughts

Verity

Three months later

"What the hell," I muttered as I shouldered my truck door open and practically fell out.

Then I stopped, sent a quick text to Randi, my best friend, to let her know where I was in case someone decided to kidnap me, and headed for the door.

"This place has got to be in the worst part of town," I muttered to myself as I walked to the door of the house and knocked.

No one answered.

I checked my phone, double checking the address, and frowned.

This place looked like a house.

In fact, if I had to guess where to get drugs in the small town of

Mooresville, Alabama, it would be on Stark Street, where I was currently standing.

"Fuck me," I grumbled, backed away, and turned to survey my surroundings.

There was a driveway on one side of the porch, and a small walkway on the other.

Going down the steps, I made my way to the walkway, and froze when I saw the bike directly next to the house.

It was pretty.

Though, it was missing a seat, and my heart started to pound.

It couldn't be.

Carefully making my way past the huge motorcycle, I started walking, and that's when I heard it.

Hammering.

In fact, I would say it sounded more like metal smashing against metal. Like someone was pounding something into submission.

Kind of like a bladesmith.

Smiling, I started to hurry in the direction of the noise, knowing I had to be in the right place.

My dad might have his dream birthday present after all.

My first mistake was not preparing myself.

The moment I saw the motorcycle, I should've known. Should've seen what was happening.

But I didn't and I fucked up.

I allowed myself to think that I was invincible, and I wasn't.

My heart, the thing that was still half broken but healing every day, started to pound the minute I pushed open the door to the shed-like thing at the back of the property, where the hammering was the loudest.

At first, it took time for my eyes to adjust, but once they did, boy oh boy were they rewarded.

There was a man standing with his back to me, one hand had a large hammer in it, and the other hand a long piece of glowing hot steel.

He was swinging the hammer at the metal, and each time he did, his muscles would flex.

When it would hit, the same muscles would bunch and release before he repeated the process all over again.

He was sweaty, too. Oh, so sweaty.

And he had a beard. From what little of it I could see, it was a magnificent one, too.

I bet he could do good things with that beard…

He turned, giving me a side view of his face, and I gasped.

I knew that beard!

I knew that face!

I'd ridden that beard!

It'd been buried between my thighs.

Oh, sweet Jesus.

I had to get out of there.

Turning, I was about to run back the way I came when the movement caught Truth's attention, and he turned fully.

We both froze, staring at each other.

Then his mouth tipped up into a leering grin, and he said, "If it isn't Ms. Very."

I pursed my lips.

Very had been something he'd called me from the moment we woke up the next morning. After all of the riding and burying.

"H-hey," I mumbled. "I was…"

"Leaving?" he guessed.

I straightened my spine and shook my head. "Uh, no."

I never, for the life of me, expected to see the last man I slept with hammering something as I walked inside, but there was a first for everything.

The man sent shivers down my spine.

I'd done my best to ignore everyone and everything when they asked about that man they saw me leaving the wedding with that night all those months ago.

Why? Because I still yearned for him.

I still wanted to ride that beard like I did that night and smother myself in his scent.

"You're a blacksmith?" I asked in confusion.

Had I even asked him what he did for a living?

He turned back to his work, picking up exactly where he'd left off when he first saw me.

Only this time, he was turned so he could see me out of the corner of his eye.

"Bladesmith," he muttered, still not taking his eyes off of what he was hammering. "Different set of training, and different set of skills are required to do the two."

"But you can do a blacksmith's work?" I continued.

Why was I prolonging this?

The answer was an easy one. The man was sexy.

Hot, sweaty. His head was dripping sweat down his neck, and it was disappearing into the collar of his shirt.

His gray shirt was wet all the way down to his waistband where you could see the different shades of grey.

"Yep," he confirmed. "I was a blacksmith before I started to hone my skills into doing this for a living."

"Do you ever worry that your beard if going to catch on fire?" I asked before I could stop myself.

He stopped what he was doing and leaned up, picking up the piece of metal and shoving it back into the burning hot coals.

"No," he admitted. "Should I?"

I shrugged.

"Those sparks are bouncing everywhere…I was just curious."

He grinned, and I watched as a drop of sweat dripped down from his hairline, around the curve of his eye, down the side of his nose, and then dropped onto the floor among a ton of similar drops just like the one that'd just landed.

When I looked back up again, it was to realize that his eyes were still on me.

"I wasn't sure this was the place I was looking for," I continued babbling. "You should put a sign out front."

He shrugged, and then pulled the metal back out of the coals.

This time it was glowing bright yellow.

"Have you ever touched that before?" I questioned.

He set the metal down onto the metal anvil like thing, and then lifted one arm.

I saw a nasty looking scar right above his right elbow, which happened to be the only thing not inked on one arm.

"Ouch," I murmured.

"What are you looking for?" he asked as he picked his hammering back up.

I fished a piece of paper out of my pocket, and unfolded it.

"A couple of months ago, my dad told me he wanted one of these. But I haven't been able to find it anywhere that didn't come from the other side of the world. And not cost my firstborn child in shipping," I murmured, walking towards him and his hammer.

The one in his hands, not the one in his pants.

His eyes shot to me, and he looked at my belly like I was about to announce something that clearly wouldn't have appealed to him, and I waved him off.

"I don't actually have any children," I admitted. "So you can wipe that panicked look off your face."

He shrugged without apology.

"A Roman sword?" he asked. "Why that?"

"My dad is a big history buff," I explained. "We visited Rome last year, and he fell in love with everything over there, especially this sword that is supposed to be an exact replica of the first Roman sword ever made."

He nodded his head, then went back to hammering.

"What are you making right now?" I asked, leaning closer.

He moved me with his hip and said, "Don't get that close. You're not wearing protection."

I bit my lip, my mind automatically going back to other protection that he'd worn.

And then I cursed myself.

Get your mind out of the gutter, Verity!

I stepped back and gave him the space that he needed, and saw a chair in the corner of the room.

Thinking that I'd just left my workout and I was on the closer end to being exhausted than not, I took a seat and waited for him to finish.

***

Truth

I hadn't expected that.

Well, I had been expecting someone.

Two someones, actually. But not this particular someone.

Finishing up the last bit of shaping for the latest blade I was forging, I thrust it into the cold water at my feet and then turned to survey the woman.

Verity, aka Very.

The woman who I'd slept with almost three months to the day ago and still masturbated to almost every single night.

She'd gotten skinnier, but not by much.

I would say she looked better, but I'd be lying.

I was quite fond of the curves she had before, but this new look, the more toned ass, and the yoga pants slicked over it—well, I kind of was into this look, too.

"What was the cost of the sword to have it made over there and shipped?" I asked, stripping my leather apron off and laying it against the table next to my hammer.

"A couple grand…" she hesitated. "Well, to be exact, it was

around twelve thousand dollars, three of it was the shipping."

I blinked.

"I can probably make that one for you for around five, but it's not going to be quick," I admitted. "I have about six ahead of you, and four of them are big projects."

She shrugged. "That's okay. Are you thinking before Christmastime, at least?"

I walked to the wall where my calendar—one of naked women from the waist up—and flipped through the months.

"You have about two and a half months until Christmas, and I expect these next builds to take me right on in to January…but I'll see what I can do. I'm not promising anything," I informed her. "Likely, I'll overshoot January, too. But we'll see."

She blinked, then nodded in understanding. "I'd like to add my name to the list."

My mouth kicked up in a semblance of a smile.

Then my first appointment showed.

Causing me to grimace.

"Yo!"

Verity jumped and turned only her head to look at the door that was at her back, and immediately stood.

"I should go," she said hastily.

"Don't worry about it," I told her. "I'm sure you remember Eugene."

Verity grimaced and waved.

Eugene was the spitting image of Kenneth. Seeing as they were twins, it wasn't unheard of.

"H-hi, Verity," Eugene looked apologetic. "I didn't know you were going to be here."

Verity shrugged her shoulders. "I didn't either."

Eugene offered her a shy smile, and I felt sorry for the both of them.

"Eugene isn't the asshole that his brother is," I told her. "Though, I'm sure you already know that. In secret, Eugene likes to tattle on his brother and slur his name."

Verity snorted.

"I know," she snickered. "I was on the receiving end of that one. And for the record, Eugene, I should've listened to you."

My brows rose and Verity was quick to explain.

"Eugene here tried to talk me out of marrying Kenneth," she smiled. "Though, I guess, technically, I did listen. I didn't marry him, after all."

Eugene smiled and moved further into the room, stopping at the table closer to me than Verity, and it was then that I saw what was really going on.

Eugene had a thing for her, but since she'd been with his brother, he'd put what he felt on the backburner.

And sadly, I became irrationally jealous over the fact that they had something that Verity and I did not.

We had one night of great sex, but Verity and Kenneth had been together for over a year. Eugene had to have known her a whole lot better than I did.

And I didn't like that.

Not one single freakin' bit.

"You want to go to lunch with us?" I asked, moving closer to her.

She blinked, looked from Eugene to me, and then nodded.

"Sure."

"Weren't you supposed to meet the girl who shall not be named?" Eugene said his first complete sentence since he'd gotten there.

That'd actually been the reason Eugene had come over. He was my scapegoat. The man that I was going to tell Destiny that I was heading to lunch with.

And what better way to get the fuck away from her with the man already here?

"Yeah," I picked up my phone that was on the table by the door. "But I can just leave her shit outside."

"Isn't it her birth certificate and social security card?" Eugene started to snort, but when he saw that I was serious, he sobered. "You have to wait. You can't leave stuff like that out on the porch. Anyone could take it."

I rolled my eyes.

"Always the Boy Scout," I mumbled. "I gotta take a shower anyway. I'll do that, and you can wait for the devil to come, and you can give her her shit."

"Who's the devil?" Verity asked as she got up off her chair.

I looked down at her, my gaze momentarily getting lost in her eyes.

"Uhh," I said as I came to the back steps. "Destiny."

Verity blinked.

"You still let her come over here?" she asked incredulously.

I shrugged. "The day I caught her cheating on me, I kicked her out. I've been slowly going through everything, and if she wants it, she comes to get it on Thursday before the trash goes out on Friday.

Most of the time I leave it by the curb, and she has to beat off the people that go through it. She asked specifically for her passport, birth certificate, and social security card, though. And I'm not that much of an ass, even though ol' Eugene here thinks otherwise."

Eugene held up his hand, but stopped from following us inside.

"Got a call. Give me a few." He held up his finger and put his phone to his ear.

Verity followed me inside, stopping short when I did.

"When he gets inside, will you tell him where these are?" I asked.

She nodded her head, and I touched the tip of my index finger to the tip of her nose.

Fuck, she looked good.

And those yoga capri pants were doing wonderful things to her ass.

The top wasn't anything too fancy, just a black racerback tank that was tight around her bust and shoulders.

The bottom was clinging to her slightly rounded belly, and I found myself remembering what it was like to run my lips down the soft skin of her navel.

"Shower?"

I blinked, coming back to the present to find Verity staring at me with a knowing look in her eyes.

"Yeah," I murmured. "Be back."

I stripped my shirt off next to the couch, and didn't miss the swift inhalation from the woman behind me.

With a smile on my face, I headed to my bathroom, stripping as I went.

By the time I got to the shower, I was naked but for my boxer briefs, which I pushed off not seconds later.

Turning on the shower, I got in, thankful for the cold water.

I needed a new water heater. Had needed one for months now.

But I hadn't gotten it yet, because showering in cold water kept me from masturbating to the sight of Verity coming every two hours.

I hadn't taken a warm shower since that night in Vegas when I'd taken her there, hot water scalding my back as I did.

I heard someone knock, and I rinsed off the soap, hastily got out, and grabbed a towel off the rack as I did.

My bathroom was small, but it wasn't nearly as small anymore now that I didn't have to contend with all of Destiny's bras, makeup, and hair products.

It was nice to be able to take a shower without having to remove everything from the shower beforehand.

In fact, I would almost claim that I…

"What are you doing here?" Destiny's annoying voice came through my paper-thin walls. "This is my house, bitch!"

I wrapped the towel around my waist, and yanked the door open to the bathroom, not stopping until I was through the bedroom door, and stalking up behind Verity who was blocking the entrance with her body.

"I'm not sure what you mean. From my understanding, this is Truth's house, correct?" Verity asked ever so sweetly.

Destiny's eyes filled with rage.

Then her mouth turned up into a smirk.

"You just like having my sloppy seconds?" Destiny mouthed off.

Verity didn't even stiffen.

"It seems like I got the better end of the stick with this one," Verity said, pressing her back against my still-wet chest. "I've, of course, had them both. What I can't understand, though, is why you would go to Kenneth when you have something like this."

She ran her hand up the side of my chest possessively.

And whether it was just for show or not, it was enough to make my semi-hard on—the one that came on the instant I realized that Verity was close—to steel pipe hardness in a matter of milliseconds.

I ground my cock into her ass, forgetting momentarily that Eugene was somewhere in the house behind us, and the she witch was in front of us…frothing at the mouth because she felt like Verity slighted her somehow.

You know, by taking her boyfriend or something.

Bitch.

"Did you need anything else?"

Verity's voice was breathy, like I was affecting her just as much as she was affecting me.

"Yes," she snapped. "I came here to talk to Truth."

"From what I understand, y'all have nothing to talk about. Just like I have nothing to talk to Kenneth about, correct?"

God, she sounded so prim and proper that I wanted to strip the pants from her lower half and fuck that proper right out of her.

But then Destiny had to go and open her mouth, reminding me that she was there when I didn't want her to be.

I'd much rather have Verity on her back, or her legs high in the air, while I drilled my cock inside of her.

Destiny could listen outside, though. That might make her being here worth it.

A smile crossed over my face, and I sighed.

"What else were you needing, Destiny?" I asked, letting my hand trail up Verity's thigh.

My hand went up to the high waistband of her pants, under her shirt, to come to a rest right where the silky smoothness of her belly met the smooth, moisture-wicking fabric.

Her belly was slightly indented where her tight pants met her skin, and I fingered the line as I waited for Destiny to speak.

Destiny, however, was busy staring at me like I'd grown a second head.

"You'd take this," she hissed, holding her hand out to encompass Verity's body. "Over this?"

She pointed at herself, and I let my eyes take Destiny in for the first time.

"Turns out I don't like skin and bones anywhere near as much as I like a girl with a little meat on her, and the confidence to pull it off," I told her. "Not to mention she's got some padding for my thighs when I take her hard from…"

Verity's hand came over my mouth, raising her shirt up slightly and allowing Destiny to see where I had my hand.

When she was confident I'd gotten the point, she let her hand drop, and I bent forward to drop a kiss on her hair.

"Turns out, you did us both a favor," Verity finally said. "If you and Kenneth hadn't cheated, we wouldn't be together." Verity crossed her hands, and I let the tips of my fingers dip into the seam of her pants, my fingers just brushing her pubic hair, causing her breath to hitch with what she said next. "Now, unless you have something pressing—like a matter of life or death—we have things to do."

Destiny's mouth thinned.

"Whatever." She snatched the papers that I just realized were on the floor where likely she'd dropped them, and started stomping down the steps to a car.

"You know," Verity murmured softly, "Kenneth bought that car for me as my wedding present." She started to laugh, making the soft skin of her belly jump. "I wonder if she realizes that she's driving in a car that I picked out."

"She got married in your wedding dress," I said as I backed up, reluctantly letting my hand fall from her belly. "Do you think she'd care if she was driving your car?"

Verity closed the door, and I watched as she took a deep breath before saying, "According to my grandmother, GG—who had no part in what happened with my wedding dress—she wasn't very happy at all to know that it was mine at one point. She only wore it because Kenneth 'supposedly' picked it out."

Her back had stiffened at the mention of her wedding dress, and I thought that our moment had fled, so I fought with myself to get my need under control.

"Where's Eugene?" I asked roughly, pushing the heel of my hand down over my cock, which incidentally was tenting the front of my towel.

"He's still on the phone," she murmured, finally turning around and allowing her eyes to meet mine.

That's when I saw the same need swirling in the depths as her eyes as I felt inside my own body.

The moment I knew she was in just as deep as me, I took a quick step forward, and pinned her to the wall with my body.

She gasped, opening her mouth to me, and I took full advantage, plunging my tongue inside and kissing the shit out of her.

She moaned, her hands curling around my shoulders, as her fingernails dug in deep.

Her leg hitched up, and I latched onto it with one palm, pushed up, and pulled out, before pressing my cock deeply into her.

Her breath hitched, her eyes closed, and I slowly started to circle my hips.

"I remember this," she breathed. "I don't remember much else we did…but this…this I could never forget."

I growled and circled my arm around her lower back, and picked her up.

She rounded my hips with both of her legs, hooking her feet at my back, causing me to lose the towel in the process.

Completely forgetting about everything—my open bedroom window, my cousin somewhere in the house or outside my house, hell even the fact that I left the forge on in my workshop—all of those things didn't matter as I brought myself down to the bed after kicking the door shut, and insinuating my hips in between Verity's thighs.

Her mouth was sweet and hot on mine as we both started to yank off her clothes.

She took her shirt off, while I took off her ridiculously too tight pants.

Her panties, which I vaguely noticed were black, were the last to go as I dropped back down onto her, my cock automatically seeking the part of her labia that would allow me to sink into her.

She moaned the moment my cock touched her overheated skin.

Goddamn, but she felt like an inferno as I slowly started to ground down into her.

"I'm on birth control this time," she breathed, causing my eyes to move up from where we were touching down below to her face.

"I'm clean," I murmured. "Had myself checked after Vegas."

Her face flushed a pretty shade of red, and she bit her lip before saying, "Me, too."

I growled and pulled back, dropping down until I could pull her pretty dusky pink nipple into my mouth.

My hand, even as large as it was, couldn't curve around her breast completely. All I was able to do was cup it, offering it to my mouth, and groaning as she started to lift her hips with each lick and suck on my part.

"God," she breathed, her hands going up to latch onto the headboard.

I'd bought a new bed after the Destiny/Kenneth fiasco.

After realizing that not even my bike was sacred to them, I had to get everything replaced that I thought might have seen some horizontal time on their part.

And having Verity in my bed, the first one to break it in, meant something to me.

Three months, ninety-two days to be exact, had gone by, and not one of those nights did I not palm my cock in this new bed of mine and think about her.

Reality was much better.

Especially with the way her pussy seemed to lunge for my fingers the moment I had them poised at her entrance.

"Please," she mewled.

I smiled happily against her nipple, then switched to the other side, giving it the same treatment that the other one had received.

She growled in frustration, her hand going to her own pussy, as she thrust her fingers inside of her right past my own.

I grinned, pinching her nipple between two teeth, before pulling back slightly to look into her eyes.

Her breath caught, and she stared at me as I pushed my finger inside, alongside hers.

"You feel good," I told her, taking a lash at her hardened nipple with the tip of my tongue.

Her eyes closed, and her neck arched, as I dropped down even lower, taking my first ever sober look at what was mine.

She moved her hand away, and was rewarded as I pulled her clit straight into my mouth and sucked.

One finger turned to two, and suddenly I was wearing her thighs as earmuffs.

Her thighs were strong, but I didn't seem to notice as I tried not to dry hump the bed with my need to take her already.

My fingers thrust and my tongue flicked.

When her pussy tightened, I knew she was about to go.

And that's when I pulled completely away, causing her to scream in frustration.

"Truth!" she cried out angrily.

"Call me by my name, baby," I settled between her thighs, guiding my cock to her entrance.

"And what's that?" she breathed.

I knew I was about to make her smile when I whispered my name in her ear. "But only say it in your head, because if you say it aloud, people might hear you."

"What are you…"

I thrust inside of her, shoving all of my hard, thick inches to the hilt.

She screamed as her orgasm poured over her, pulling her under as she writhed and squirmed underneath of me.

I held still while she rode it out, and was just about to start moving again when I heard it.

"Uhh, guys?" Eugene called through the door. "I'll just head on home, if that's okay."

I smiled against Verity's mouth. "You do that, Eugene."

I heard the door close moments later, and I started moving my hips once again; slow, smooth movements that had my balls drawing up within seconds.

Then I heard Eugene talking again outside my open bedroom window.

"You need to go home," Eugene ordered. "And preferably not come back."

That's when I heard Destiny's voice reply, but my balls chose that moment to empty, and I shot everything I had inside of the best pussy I'd ever had in my life.

CHAPTER 4

*I'm not saying she's a hoe, but she's taken more
loads than a washing machine.*

-Verity to Truth upon discussion of Truth's ex

Verity

My vagina was pleasantly sore, and I found myself following
behind Truth and his seatless motorcycle thirty minutes after the
best sex of my life—that I could actually remember.

I was sure all the orgasms he gave me while in Vegas were pretty
amazing, too. Yet, I couldn't remember much more than vague
impressions of greatness from that twenty-four hours.

We arrived at the restaurant he said was the best place in four cities
surrounding our little town, and I opened my car door just as he
walked up to my car.

"I'm not really sure that riding seatless is altogether safe," I told
him. It'd been something I'd thought about the entire way here,
and my mouth didn't know how not to blurt shit out.

He grinned.

"Riding a motorcycle isn't the safest thing in the world to do, yet
you see me still riding, don't you?" he teased, offering me his
elbow. "If you put aside your dreams in lieu of safety, or comfort,

what will that accomplish? Not much. Because in the end you'll be unhappy. But hey! You'll be safe!"

I pinched his side and fell into step beside him, my arm hitched up high and tight to the side of his chest.

"You're incredibly tall," I mumbled. "And one of your strides are two of mine."

He immediately slowed down, not that I was telling him to. I'd only been making conversation.

I was a nervous chatter box when I was in a position where I felt that silence wasn't the best option.

Such as now, walking into Truth's favorite restaurant.

"Six foot four and some change," he answered as he opened the door with his free hand.

You know, the one that wasn't currently pinning mine to his chest.

"Thank you," I whispered as I walked inside.

The bright sunlight from outside made it impossible for my eyes to adjust immediately when we entered the darkened pub. But the moment they did, I gasped.

"Holy shit!" I breathed. "This is like a real Irish pub."

Truth chuckled at my back and moved me forward, finally letting go of me, but not for long.

Settling his hand on the small of my back, he guided me forward to a hostess stand.

He didn't stop, though.

Instead, he grabbed his own drink menu, a couple of kids coloring mats, two sets of crayons, and showed me to a table all on his own.

"You're allowed to just seat yourself here?" I asked in confusion.

The pub wasn't empty. In fact, I would say it was almost packed.

Every single table except for a booth on the far west wall, and a couple of tables interspersed throughout the room, were taken.

He led me to the bar, though.

There was a little section with high top tables and stools to the side of it that was set apart from the rest of the restaurant. It was closer to the kitchen—which was quite noisy. It wasn't the most ideal place, nor one that I would've picked on my own.

But this was his favorite restaurant, so I bowed down to his desires. Even if they were unorthodox.

"Yep," he finally answered as he pulled my stool away from the bar top. "I know the owner."

"So…" I said the moment he sat down. "Your real name is Ernest?"

Truth's eyes narrowed.

"I wasn't kidding about sharing that," he informed me. "If it gets out, I know just who to come to when I hear it."

I held up my hand in the universal sign of promise. "Vulcan's honor."

He snorted and picked up the menu.

"What are you getting?" I asked. "Since it's your favorite restaurant and all."

"The special," he answered. "I was just trying to see what there was for an appetizer. I can hear your stomach growling from all the way over here."

I grinned.

"I started these shake/meal replacement type things a few weeks ago, and I drink it for breakfast and sometimes lunch if I'm having a bad day," I explained. "This'll be the first time I've gone out to eat since I started them. I'll have to try to eat healthy."

Truth grunted something unintelligible, and before I could ask him what that grunt was supposed to mean, an old man who looked to be in his mid-seventies walked up to the table and placed his large, frail hand on top of Truth's head.

"There's my boy," the old man said.

His voice was still loud and boisterous, despite his hunched over position and frail body.

And now that I was looking at him, I could see the resemblance between the two men.

It must be his grandfather. Their ears were exactly the same, and you could really tell seeing as Truth shaved his head, and the old man had no hair to speak of.

The old man, however, did have an amazing beard. One that hung nearly all the way down to his navel.

It was snow white on the top, and faded from white to grey to black at the ends.

It was the most unusual beard I'd ever seen, and I found myself wanting to sneak my phone out of my purse to send a picture to Randi.

She would definitely understand the majesty that was this beard.

"What can I get you, boy?" the old man asked.

I couldn't place his accent.

I'd heard something similar, but I wasn't sure if it was Irish, Scottish, or English.

It was thick at times, and not so thick at others.

"A draft, an order of cheese fries, and I'm going to have the special," Truth answered. "What are you going to have, Very?"

I blushed and opened my menu, and chose the first thing that I saw that looked excellent.

"Uhh," I murmured, looking at the old man who was scrutinizing me like one would a potential adversary. "I'll have the special number two and a sweet tea, please."

The old man nodded.

"All right, Nessie. I'll be back."

Then the man walked away without looking back, but did it so slowly that I worried he'd even make it to the kitchen.

I shouldn't have worried.

He never had any intentions of going to the kitchen.

The second he reached the end of the bar, he took a seat, and then bellowed out the orders to a passing waitress, who nodded her head and went to a computer without another word.

I blinked.

Then smiled.

"That's healthy?" he teased.

"You put me on the spot. I wasn't sure what to order," I shrugged. "I'm never going to be a small girl," I finally admitted. "In fact, losing all this weight is a fluke."

His eyes darkened. "I happen to love the curves you have just fine," he told me bluntly. "I gotta say, you look real nice, but Jesus. That dress you were in at the wedding…that was my dream girl right there."

My mouth twitched.

"I still have all those curves, but I just try to keep them all contained."

His mouth thinned.

"If you ever want to let them out to play again, you know where I am," he finally said. "Not to mention I'm fairly positive that those capri pants you're wearing come in at a close second to the dress."

I huffed out a laugh.

"They're definitely something that I struggle to get on every day," I told him matter of factly. "But they make my ass look good, so I keep slicking them on even though they cut off circulation to my calves."

He snorted just as our appetizer was set down on the table in front of us, and I did nothing but stare.

"Holy shit," I murmured. "That's…big."

He chuckled and picked up his fork, setting the napkin that it had been rolled in on his lap, causing me to squeal inside.

My GG would love him.

I was fairly sure if she'd been there with us, and had seen him place his napkin on his lap, she would've stared at me with 'marry him now' eyes.

As it was, I knew that my GG was going to give me the third degree the moment I got home.

I'd seen her as we were driving out of town, and I knew she was paying attention to the man on the seatless bike who I was trailing behind.

She'd put two and two together, and likely get way more than it was ever supposed to be.

But that was my GG. A pain in my ass and my first best friend.

GG had been the woman who had practically raised me, and the moment that she suspected I was about to find a man, she'd be there, ready to inspect him.

"You gonna eat any of this?"

I looked down to see nearly half of the plate of cheese fries gone, and Truth looking at me with upraised brows.

Picking up my fork and placing the napkin on my lap, I took a hesitant bite, and moaned.

"Oh, my God," I gasped. "This is white cheese sauce…and it's perfect."

It was, too.

It was the best thing I'd ever tasted in my life.

Fries. Bacon. Cheese sauce. *Bacon.* Ranch.

What more could a person ask for in life?

Apparently, the answer to that was more cheese, because the moment Truth's grandfather came back over thirty seconds later, he was appalled to see how little cheese sauce we had, even though the plate was already overflowing with it.

"More, more, more!" he ordered at the first waitress he saw. "And bacon."

The waitress nodded and disappeared, leaving us with a glaring grandfather standing beside the table.

"Why didn't you say anything, boyo?"

Truth's smile was fierce.

"I thought maybe you were trying to slim me down," he challenged, leaning back and letting his work-roughened hand trail down his taut belly.

"Introduce me, boyo."

Truth grinned.

"This is my grandfather," Truth said, then pointed to me. "Pop, this is Verity. My woman."

"Nice to meet you, Truth's woman."

Then 'Pop' rolled his eyes and walked away.

"Your grandfather is…festive," I laughed.

Truth snorted.

"I…"

Then everything went to hell.

The doors to the pub burst open, and two men, both carrying baseball bats, came inside bellowing about dues.

Before I even knew what was going on, Truth was on his feet and rounding the curve of the bar and heading straight for the two men, who looked extremely upset.

Truth arrived in front of the two men just as a large man arrived. A man dressed completely in black.

The man in black looked like he was a freakin' mob boss with his black hair, black clothes, black shoes, and dark eyes.

Truth, though he had the same tall, dark and dangerous vibe going on, didn't look like he was going to kill the two men.

At least not until they took two threatening steps in the direction of his grandfather, then he looked murderous.

"No."

Just one word from Truth's mouth had both men halting in their steps.

"We…"

"This is a place of business," Truth snapped. "You need to leave, or I'll have you thrown out."

"You're not the owner. Only the owner can do that."

Truth laughed in their faces.

"My grandfather owns this bar, and I'm his beneficiary," he told them bluntly. "There's literally nothing that I can't do here, besides fire people. But that's only because Pop hates hiring new help."

The two men said nothing.

The mob boss at Truth's side, however, had something to say.

"Get. Out," he ordered. "Or I'll make you get out."

Between Truth and the mob boss lookalike, the two men came to their senses and backed out.

But not before he pointed at Truth's grandfather, promising retaliation despite not saying a word.

"Out!" Truth's grandfather bellowed.

Definitely Irish.

The more upset or animated he got, the more the accent appeared.

Noted.

Truth walked to the door and watched the two men, while I sat in my spot and contemplated asking him if he was related to the Irish mob.

By the time he retook his seat, I realized that he was too upset and pissed off to broach the subject.

Maybe tomorrow when he didn't look like he could crush the beer bottle he was holding with one hand.

This scary, pissed off Truth was actually quite appealing. However, I didn't continue to chatter because I knew he didn't want to hear my overactive mouth talking. Not at that moment, anyway.

So I sat there, in silence, while he tried to compose himself.

Which took all the way until our food was brought over.

"Wow," I murmured. "You weren't kidding. It's huge."

His mouth twitched as he picked up his knife and fork.

"I think you said that our first night together, too."

I snorted a laugh, and then enjoyed the most scrumptious steak I'd ever had in my life.

CHAPTER 5

I'm all about meaningful things in life: sex, ass grabs, surprise candy bars, and kisses.

-Verity's secret thoughts

Verity

You know those people who go to the gym and you just know that they're not really there to work out?

Those girls who prance around smiling in their cute little leggings with the perfectly cut holes in the thighs with the matching little sports bra, with their perfectly made up faces and perfectly coiffed hair?

"You can't trust them," I told Randi as sweat dripped down my face. "They're not here to work out. I don't think I've seen that one," I pointed to a brunette with tits the size of cantaloupes, "do a single thing but flirt with that guy by the bench press machine."

"That guy's gay," Randi observed as she sucked back her water in between pants. "I wonder if she knows she's barking up the wrong tree."

I placed the weights down, and spun around so I wasn't facing the mirror, scrutinizing the play-by-play between the two in front of us.

"That woman is under the impression that she can get him anyway," I surmised as I realized what I was seeing. "That's Tessie. She's a bitch and she knows exactly who that man is. I take a class with both of them, and the majority of the time he comes in with his boyfriend, Todd."

Randi sighed. "Why am I here with you if you take a boot camp in the morning?"

Because I didn't want to get fat…or fatter.

"You know why," I told her, spinning around and returning to my set.

Today was arm day.

I was doing three sets of ten on the bench press. Curls, triceps, and butterflies before I walked another two miles around the track outside that circled the building.

"I know, but you've already lost a good twenty pounds since the wedding. You look good. I don't see why you're trying as hard as you are."

I didn't, either.

Only that working out had been the turning point that got me through a lot of lows. Canceling trips to Hawaii were hard when the trips were being utilized at the time.

Then there was the hotel stays and car rentals. Venues and other fun stuff that I had to get my money back on.

So yes, it'd been a trying few months, and working out had been the balm that soothed my soul and kept me from eating when I got frustrated.

Though, I had a lot of appreciation for my trainer, Emily.

She was the bomb and encouraged me to try my hardest even when I didn't think I had anything left.

"Whoa," Randi said in surprise. "The best-looking beard I've seen on the continent of North America just walked in here. Oh, and look! Your girl just left the gay dude. She's in hot pursuit."

I turned, ready to see this beard, and froze.

"That's Truth," I murmured softly.

Softly enough that I wouldn't bring attention to my position.

Maybe if I didn't move, he wouldn't notice my bright neon green yoga capris that were likely stained with sweat around my ass.

"I know it's the truth," Randi said. "I called it first."

I rolled my eyes.

Randi and I played a game. It was simple, really. The first one to call the beard—kind of like a game of slug bug—got to punch the other.

I held up my hand when she reared back.

"No," I stopped her. "That's *Truth*," I hissed. "The man I slept with."

Her eyes widened, and she threw a hand over her mouth to stifle the scream.

"Oh, my God," she gasped. "The man that rocked your socks off?"

I nodded my head.

"That's the one."

She moved to stand in front of me, and gestured for me to finish my set with a wave of her hand.

I laid down and picked up the bar, thinking about the man who was likely getting the brunette gym bunny's phone number.

Maybe he'd at least call her back.

I couldn't say the same consideration had been afforded to me.

He hadn't responded to any of my calls or messages. In fact, this was the first time I'd seen him in a week. He was a wham, bam, thank you ma'am kind of man, I supposed. Apparently, he just didn't feel like talking. Whatever the case, I would ignore him.

"Does my hair look terrible," I breathed through a rep.

Randi looked at my hair, then lied like the good friend she was.

"It looks perfect."

I snorted.

I could feel the sweat causing my hair to stick to my forehead, and I could see the colored strands of my purple highlights in my peripheral vision every time I moved my head a certain way.

It was apparent that my braid was coming undone whether I wanted it to or not.

And Truth was going to see me.

There was no way around it.

The gym we were in was small, and one of the only ones in the city of Mooresville.

It was either work out here, or at home, and I hadn't seen any weights in Truth's small house or workshop.

I should've known that he'd be here at some point; especially with the amount of time I spent here.

"You have four more, and then we can go, right?" she asked.

Randi knew all about Truth.

I'd told her all about our first time, and then again seven days ago when it'd happened for the second time.

Randi, of course, had informed me that I needed to drive over to his house.

I, on the other hand, told her that had he wanted me there, he would've answered one of my many phone calls or texts.

I nodded my head at my best friend, then pushed myself to finish my last four reps.

By the time I was finished, I had even more sweat all over my face, and I was fairly sure I was about to die.

"Ohhh," Randi breathed. "Here he comes."

Then she leaned forward and covered my face by standing with my head underneath her thighs. Inches away from her vagina.

"Uhh," I said to her vagina. "I don't think this is necessary."

She reached between her legs and placed her hand over my mouth. "Shhh, it feels weird when you're talking to my vagina and not me."

I started laughing then and pushed her away.

"Go," I said. "Breathing in your vagina fumes crosses all kinds of boundaries that are best not crossed."

She smacked me just as Truth stopped what he was doing, which was curling a fifty-pound dumbbell.

The minute he realized that one of the two weirdos was me, he re-racked the weights and turned to face me.

"Where, exactly, have you been?"

My brows rose.

"I've been here. Where have you been?"

He tilted his head.

"Working," he answered again. "But, if I had your number, I would've at least tried to call you once I got off of work."

My brows rose.

"I did call you…and text you," I said. "Though, I can see how I might've forgotten to give you my number."

"You might've forgotten…" he repeated. "And you never told me where you lived. How, exactly did you expect me to get into contact with you?"

"Oh, I don't know," I said, narrowing my eyes. "How about answering one of the texts I sent."

"Were you the one who sent those one word texts four times, once each day, over the last few days?" he guessed.

I nodded my head.

"Four times," he said. "One phone call, and four texts, each of which just said 'hey.'"

I grimaced.

"Well, that was more than I got from you."

He snorted.

"I was working," he said. "And I have been for the last week because a new semester started. Not to mention it's kind of hard when I don't know it's you that was texting. Would it have killed you to say 'hey, it's Verity?'"

My brows furrowed at his words.

I sighed.

He was right.

Randi, however, was tired of being silent.

"I'm Randi." She held out her hand. "Do you have any friends with nice beards?"

I smacked my friend's arm.

"You have a husband with a nice beard," I chastised her. "And I'm pretty sure he'd take exception to you asking some stranger that."

"He's not a stranger," Randi countered. "He's obviously more than friends with you. So, about those friends."

I sighed.

"You're off the hook. You can go eat now."

She looked torn.

I knew how much she detested the gym, and only came because she was a nice, supportive friend.

However, she'd been telling me about the tacos her husband had started making since we'd started the workout, and I knew she was ready to get home and eat them.

Hell, I was ready to eat them and I hadn't even been invited.

"Fine," she finally settled on. "But I'll be hearing everything there is to hear tomorrow, understand?"

With that she left, leaving the two of us standing in an uncomfortable silence.

"What else do you do besides working on your bladesmith stuff?" I asked him, circling one finger around the braid of my hair and twirling it as I waited for a response.

"I'm a firearms instructor and police academy instructor," he answered. "How much longer do you have until you're done?"

I hadn't known.

I thought that he only worked on his blades. It was news to me that he had another job on top of that one.

"Umm," I hesitated. "I was going to go walk outside…to catch Pokémon."

His mouth twitched. "How long will that take you?"

I looked at my watch. "About an hour or so. Why?"

He nodded once.

"That gives me enough time to finish up here, and then you can go with me to dinner."

I pursed my lips.

"What makes you think I want to go to dinner with you?" I asked.

He leaned in close, and was about an inch away from touching his mouth to mine when we were interrupted.

"Um, excuse me," a hesitant, sugary sweet voice called from behind us. "But would you mind showing me how to use this machine?"

I turned.

Truth, however, was not deterred from his goal.

His hand hooked around my chin, turned my face to his, and then I could taste him.

He'd had something pepperminty, and I could taste it on his tongue.

His beard tickled my jaw, and it took everything I had not to collapse in a puddle of goo at his feet.

Then he released me, and went back to his weights.

I stood there, watching him with a dumbfounded expression on my face, and ogled while he lifted.

He'd gotten to the number ten when he said, "Those Pokémon won't catch themselves."

I jumped.

"I'll be outside."

Then I ran away, trying not to let my vagina do the thinking.

Because if I did let her out to play, I'd be doing him in the freakin' locker room, and he was right.

Those Pokémon wouldn't catch themselves, and I had an egg about to hatch.

***

He found me outside an hour later, and I was staring at the screen of my phone with a determined look on my face.

"Come on, you little fucker," I grumbled, tossing another ball at the piece of shit that refused to stay captured.

Hands grabbed my hips, and I gasped and spun, coming face to face with a sweaty and amused Truth.

"I called your name three times," he said, explaining why he'd scared me.

I grinned and closed my phone, shoving it into the pocket at the back of my capri pants.

He watched me do it, and grinned as he gestured toward the parking lot.

"Let's go," he said.

I followed him, resisting the urge to grab his hand, and walked side by side with him through the small garden that was outside the gym, stopping only once when the ducks from the pond tried to demand food from us.

"Where do you want to go to eat?" he asked.

I pursed my lips.

"Sushi?" I offered.

If I was going to break my diet, I might as well break it thoroughly.

He nodded once and came to a stop in front of my car.

"You can ride with me if you want," he offered.

I looked around for the familiar looking bike with no seat, and furrowed my brows.

"What are you driving?" I asked.

He pointed to another bike, this one with a seat, and I frowned.

"Did you get rid of the old one?"

"Nope," he denied. "Still sitting in the same spot I parked it after leaving dinner with you."

"Did you have this one?" I continued.

He handed me his helmet and I took it, pulling it on over my messy braid while continuing to hold eye contact.

"Yes," he answered. "But I'd sent a few pieces of the engine in to get fixed, and just got them back yesterday. It leaves a bad taste in my mouth to drive the other one."

I tilted my head to the side.

"Destiny and Kenneth are bad people," I told him. "So they did it on your bike…who cares? Just put the seat back on and ride it. It's not like you had any responsibility in why they cheated."

He gestured for me to get on, and I did, waiting for him to answer.

Reaching forward to strap my helmet on tighter, he said, "It's tainted. Everything about that bike was mine. I'd built it from the ground up. To have them do that on my bike…it left a bad taste in my mouth. It is a signal of my failure, and I didn't want to continue to see that, and be reminded of that. The bike, although it was my baby, is replaceable. Why continue to use something that doesn't make me happy anymore," he smiled evilly then. "Plus, wouldn't you stop sleeping in your bed if you found out that she was fucked by your man in it?"

I paused, my lips pursing, and sighed, "Well, actually, I did have to replace my bed. So, I do understand."

He nodded once and took his seat in front of me.

When he sat down, it was on top of my thighs, so I scooted back as far as the seat would allow me, which sadly, wasn't much.

With the two of us on this bike, I was unsure of the power.

However, the minute he started it, and I felt the power of the motor between my thighs, all doubts fled my mind.

Instead of worrying about how my ass was hanging off the back, or anything else pertaining to my ass, I wrapped my arms tightly around Truth, and let the wind take me.

And when Truth pulled up in front of the same pub, I realized that he was giving me a gift.

He was sharing his world with me, and I was going to let him.

Two hours later, I took him to my house.

Well, I gave him directions, anyway.

The moment he saw it, he stopped at the end of the driveway and stared.

"This is a big fucking house!" he yelled over the din of the motor.

I snorted.

"Call it what it is! A monstrosity!" I yelled back.

He put his foot back up onto the pedal thingy while turning the throttle with his hand, and we were off again, setting off through the gate and straight up my driveway, coming to a stop next to my car—which somehow had magically appeared.

Though, really, I knew it was Randi.

Her and her husband likely were responsible for it, and I made a mental note to thank the both of them tomorrow.

I'd do it today, but I had a feeling we were about to be very busy.

He shut off the bike and stared up at the house, his jaw going slack as he took it in.

"It's big," he murmured, holding his hand out for me to take.

I did, sweeping my leg off of the bike and staring up at the house, trying to see what he saw.

I didn't know what he saw, though.

I'd been coming to this house for my entire twenty-nine years of life, and I didn't see it as anything but home anymore.

"How many rooms does this place have?"

I gestured for him to follow me while placing the helmet on the seat he'd just vacated, and he fell in step beside me as I started to explain.

"This is what they call a Colonial," I murmured. "It has thirteen bedrooms. There are eight bathrooms, a kitchen, two living room areas, two formal dining rooms, a ballroom, and an indoor pool," I explained.

"Did the pool come original with the house?" he asked as I led him around the side of the house.

I used the back entrance instead of the front.

Mainly because I had to walk all the way through the house to get to the kitchen, and usually had groceries of some form or fashion.

Not to mention my great-grandmother always used to use this door, so it seemed only proper that I used it, too.

"No," I fished my keys out of my purse. "The pool was added during my GG's time here. She moved out a few years ago, and now she lives in the little row house next to the lake."

"There's a lake?" he turned his head to search behind him.

"Yes," I pushed the door open and led him inside, hearing him close the door securely behind me. "It's beyond the trees that you see at the end of the lawn."

"Who mows this place?" he asked.

I started to snicker.

"That would be me," I said. "Every Saturday that I'm off."

"When are you not off?" he asked as he looked around. "I haven't actually seen you work yet."

I knew what he was asking.

How the hell did I afford a place like the one I was currently living in.

"My great-grandmother was one of the original Cassidy Winemakers in Mooresville County," I started to explain.

His eyes closed, and he started to nod.

"That explains the CW on the gate," he surmised.

I smiled softly.

"When my great-grandmother died, she left my GG this place, and me a sizeable trust fund that I was able to access four years ago." I walked to the cabinet and pulled out a bottle of wine. "Want any?"

His brows rose, but he nodded anyway.

"What?" I asked.

"That bottle looks old," he murmured.

"My GG and great-grandmother were wine connoisseurs. You can't expect a person, such as my grandmother and great-grandmother, to not have wine just lying around the house."

"Touché."

I nodded firmly and handed him the bottle and the corkscrew.

He took it deftly, easily removing the cork and handing it back to me.

I placed two glasses in front of him, and he poured them not halfway like most would, but all the way up to the top.

"You know me already," I giggled. "I thought it was only Randi and me who didn't waste any time or effort when it came to wine. It's good to see you have the same thought processes."

He winked.

"The house?" he reminded me.

"My GG gave it to me three years ago when she moved out, although I've been living here for most of my life."

He nodded silently.

"Your grandmother or great-grandmother ever have any men here?" he questioned. "This is a big ass place for someone like you to run on your own."

"Yep," I confirmed. "Though my grandfather's health declined to where he couldn't help in the later years. They hired a caretaker who came out once a month to do any major repairs before he passed."

He winced, and then picked up a vase, causing me to giggle. "That's my paternal grandmother."

He set it down and backed away.

I snorted.

"I know you're wondering why my mother didn't get this place," I said. "And I'll go ahead and appease that curiosity. My mother is a squanderer. She's selfish and greedy, and that sets her up for failure which is why she is barely holding onto her wedding planning business by the skin of her teeth."

"Teeth don't have skin…" he looked up to study the kitchen

cabinets. "And your place really needs a complete remodel."

I snorted.

"Yep," I confirmed. "It needs one yesterday, but I don't have time. I work full-time for the newspaper, and when I'm not working, I'm trying to keep my mother's business in line, and stop the whole thing from imploding."

"You don't have any time for you?" he tilted his head to study me.

He was now leaning against my GG's china cabinet, and I realized how out of place he looked in front of it.

"I blow."

He blinked.

"That's good news, I guess," he drawled.

I snickered and went back out the kitchen door, and straight to the small workroom that I used to do my hobby.

"This," I said, pushing open the door, "is where I blow glass."

He looked around the room, studying everything.

"That's amazing," he finally said. "Did you make this?"

He picked up a hummingbird feeder the color of blood, and I picked up its twin.

"There are a lot of imperfections," I admitted. "And yes, I did make it."

He fingered the small stem that was where the hummingbird would feed when it was hung.

"Fuckin' amazing," he finally murmured. "I've always looked at these things and wondered how it was done. Will you show me?"

I smiled.

"Yes." I placed the feeder back on the shelf. I had to ship them out tomorrow evening. "But not tonight. Tonight, I want to eat, kick back on the couch and watch our movie. I'm exhausted."

"Why are you so tired?" he asked. "I'm not saying that you didn't kick ass at catching all those Pokémon, but you have bags under your eyes that look like you haven't slept in days."

I fingered said bags.

"It's rained the last three mornings in a row, and in the newspaper business, that's not a good thing," I told him. "People call and complain about the stupidest things, but when it's raining, it's a relentless stream of calls that never ends."

He took my hand in his, and then led me back to the house.

"You can give me a tour of the rest of your mansion. Then you can show me what you have to cook, while you go find us something to watch on TV and I cook it," he murmured as he pulled me along behind him. "Then we can have a Netflix and chill kind of night."

I rolled my eyes. "Netflix and chill doesn't mean what you think it means."

He looked at me over his shoulder.

"I know."

That was how I found myself becoming one with my couch while Truth made me the most delicious spaghetti and meatballs I'd ever tasted.

My food normally came out tasting bland, but the spices and overall taste of Truth's sauce was something that I would remember for a long time to come.

And I would enjoy the hell out of my leftovers tomorrow during lunch.

Now we were watching *Battleship*, my most favorite movie in the world. I had a *How to Get Away With Murder* marathon planned after this movie.

"Why do you like this one so much?" he asked.

I smiled where I was at, leaning with my back to his chest, my head leaning against his collarbone.

"Because there are hot men in Navy uniforms in it," I teased. "The Navy is my favorite."

"Hmmm," he murmured. "Interesting."

I bit my lip.

I told myself not to ask, but Truth just struck me as a military man, and any information about him, even the most insignificant, I soaked up like a sponge.

"Were you in the military?" I asked.

He seemed to hesitate, and then he nodded. "Yes."

Curiosity started to get the better of me, and even though I could tell that he wanted me to drop the subject, I didn't.

Instead, I pushed.

And nearly lost Truth before I even had him.

CHAPTER 6

Ladies, just a reminder. There's always another
man out there with an extra inch more than the
one who's fucking you over.

-Fact of Life

Truth

"Were you in the military?"

Was I in the military?

Hundreds of things swirled through my mind at her question.

I should lie, because if I told the truth, then she'd want to know more.

Especially knowing that her favorite branch was the Navy.

But it wasn't the Navy that was the hard part of this discussion, it was what I did after the Navy.

A killer for hire wasn't something that most women wanted to see on the resume of the man they were interested in. Though, I guess I wasn't exactly a killer for hire, but I did a lot of killing and got paid for it.

But that was what happened in the black ops unit called Crow.

A unit I would still belong to had I not had one really bad experience that changed my life and forced me to slow down.

Though, Crow did do right by me. However, that had a lot to do with Sean, aka Seanshine, another biker and member of The Dixie Wardens. Sean had been a member of Crow with me, and after I'd nearly died, I'd gotten out, and he immediately introduced me to the Dixie Wardens.

The Dixie Wardens had taken me in, made me whole again, and in the process, had saved my life.

"Yes," I finally answered, bracing myself for the next question.

I was sure she could feel the tenseness that had slid throughout my body, but the woman was curious by nature. She was going to ask, and I prepared myself for the onslaught of questions.

"What branch?"

My belly tightened.

"The Navy."

Her gasp of surprise and delight didn't send warm flurries of excitement through me like it would've once done.

Instead, it sent dread and fear through me.

Because it was inevitable now.

She'd want to know everything.

When I got out. Why I got out. Where I went after that. What I did.

And those were all questions she asked, and I answered each and every one until the last one.

"I...it's hard to talk about." I finally settled on as an answer for her question about what I did once I got out. "I'll eventually tell you, but right now...at night...it's neither the time nor the place."

She frowned, and opened her mouth to say something, and

irrational anger surged through me.

"I gotta go," I mumbled.

Then I stood up, ignoring her cry to wait, and marched through her fancy-ass house as fast as my booted feet would take me without actually running.

Because Truth Reacher didn't run.

Not from anyone or anything.

Not even a half-pint sized woman with the ass of an angel who scared the absolute shit out of me.

I got on my bike and looked at the house one last time before leaving, not surprised to see her in the window that overlooked the carport.

She had no clue that the subject she'd touched on wasn't just a sensitive one. I'd almost lost my life.

Multiple times.

Knowing that I needed to talk to someone who knew the situation but wouldn't give me biased opinions, I rode straight to my pop's place.

And it gave me the perfect excuse to go there, because I knew he didn't want me bringing up the incident that'd taken place the last time I'd been there.

I'd meant to ask him about the incident at the bar a few days ago, but I'd been so busy with work and classes that it fell onto the back burner.

Now, though, I was done with my current work in progress, class was canceled for the night due to no electricity, and my pop's pub was closed.

It was open every single day except for Tuesdays, which was the night my Grams went to bingo.

And she would walk if she had to, but Pop never let her.

In fact, Pop loved Grams so much that he closed down his pub on Tuesdays just so he could take her. Then he went there and sat in his empty bar and waited for ten o'clock to roll around so he could go to get her.

Arriving in a matter of minutes, I parked in my usual spot right beside the door and used my key to get inside.

"Pop!" I bellowed from the entrance of the empty bar.

Pop didn't answer.

"Pop!" I called loudly. "Are you in here?"

The pub was empty, the lights were on and the jukebox was playing, but the only person in the entire place was obviously me.

Because had he been here, my pop would've answered with his usual bellow.

But when none was forthcoming, I headed out the back entrance to check to see if his car was here, and frowned when I saw that it was.

Maybe he was in the walk-in freezer.

But when I didn't see him in there, either, I started to worry.

Pulling my cell phone out of my pocket, I dialed his number and waited.

Dread slithered through me as I heard his phone going off on the bar.

He would've never left that here.

Not when Grams might call him early, because she did that sometimes. When her arthritis would start acting up, and she'd need to leave because she just couldn't hack sitting up anymore.

Walking over to the phone, I picked it up and stared at it like it was a snake about to strike.

The movement placed me close to the bar, and I could just barely see over the top to the floor behind the bar.

That's when I saw the shoe.

And the blood.

So much blood.

Too much blood.

***

"What happened?"

I turned to Big Papa and Aaron, who were staring at me like I was about to lose it, and they were there to prevent it.

"I was at my girl, Verity's, place. Then I left there and headed over here. I wanted to talk to Pop about a few things, found him like that."

My voice cracked on the word 'that' and both men chose not to notice my near breakdown.

"Anything out of place when you came in?" Big Papa pushed.

I shook my head.

"No," I denied. "Everything was normal when I first came in. Nothing out of place. Lights all on, jukebox playing softly in the corner just like Pop liked it when he was by himself. I called out his name, and he didn't answer, so I went through the back to see if I could find his car behind the building, and did. So I pulled my phone out to call, and his phone rang on top of the bar."

Big Papa's eyes looked haunted as he peered over the bar at where my grandfather's dead body lay, curled up and broken.

"Chief."

I turned to see Officer Stephanie come in, a worried look on her face.

"Yeah?" Big Papa grunted.

It was still weird to hear Big Papa called Chief, I thought numbly.

It'd been nearly a year since the old chief, and the president of The Dixie Wardens MC Alabama Chapter, Stone, was killed by a gang member.

To this day, I still found myself dialing his number only to hang up before it rang.

It was such a habit to call the man when I had problems that I didn't even realize I was doing it until it was nearly too late.

Stone had been the one to take me under his wing when I'd come home broken. He'd been the one to bring me into his life, into his home with his wife and child, giving me the time I needed to heal from my wounds—both physical and emotional.

So to hear Big Papa, Stone's VP, called 'Chief' was hard.

He still refused to go by 'President' of The Dixie Wardens. Though he technically was the president, we still called him the VP.

"Would you mind stepping outside for a moment?" Officer Stephanie asked.

I was surprised with the officer's polite demeanor.

Normally she was a ball buster, but tonight I supposed she was being nice in deference to my grandfather's murder.

She and I didn't see eye-to-eye.

She was also an instructor at the police academy, and we taught differently.

Though, that was just because she was a woman and I was a man.

We had different perspectives on certain things law enforcement wise, and that would never change.

"Okay," Big Papa said. "I'll be back. Aaron, finish up here, yeah?"

Aaron nodded and turned to stare at me.

"You're going to be okay?"

I stared at the new guy, and nodded my head.

Aaron was a good man. He was the newest member of the club and was fast becoming one of my friends.

"I don't think it's sunk in yet," I finally settled on. "I see him there, see his body…but I feel numb."

A loud curse had me looking toward the door where Stephanie had pulled Big Papa to the side.

He was staring down at her with pure rage on his face.

She continued to talk, and I stopped listening to what Aaron was saying and started focusing in on what they were discussing.

"Shit," Big Papa groaned. "Fuck."

And that's when I knew.

Stephanie had been the one to be assigned to go check on my grandmother.

And by the look on Stephanie's face, my grandmother had likely received the same fate as my grandfather.

Having it confirmed moments later was pure torture.

And that's when it finally sank in.

CHAPTER 7

In college, my favorite course was intercourse.

-Truth's secret thoughts

Truth

The first time I saw the meme floating around the Internet, I had zero to nil patience left in me.

Everything that was left was rage.

Normally, I would've handled it better.

I would've told the person who shared it on Facebook that they needed to take that meme down before I beat their ass.

Instead, I went straight to beating their ass.

Well, not the person who shared it with me, but the person who made the meme.

'Hey, isn't this you, bro?' I read again on my company's page.

But it wasn't just me who saw it.

So far, it'd been shared over a thousand times, and multiple people who I knew that were commenting or tagging me in it.

The picture wasn't that bad.

Of me, anyway.

Well, not of Verity, either.

It was the words that had me pissed off.

The picture itself was of Verity and I riding on the back of my bike, my helmet seated firmly on her head, and her hands around my waist.

It was a profile shot, but it clearly showed part of Verity's ass hanging off the back of the bike seat.

But that wasn't because she was fat, it was because the seat on that bike was on the smaller side, and really only made for one person.

Yet, the person taking the photo had no problem putting 'watch out—wide load' across the bottom of the photo right under Verity's ass.

Picking up the phone, *calmly*, I called in a favor from a friend of mine in Kilgore, Texas. A man whose wife was a computer savant that could find out anything I wanted to know with only a few minutes' effort on her part.

"Hello?" Jack answered shortly.

I could hear kids screaming in the background, and I found my first smile in two days.

Jack was a good man. I'd met him while he was deployed at the same time that I was, though he was Army and I was Navy. Usually we would've never crossed paths, but a SEAL never knew where he'd end up or what mission he'd be needed on.

Ten years later, he was married with a shit ton of kids and living about four hours away from me in a biker club of his own.

"I need help tracking down the original poster of a picture on fuckbook," I said without preamble.

I hated Facebook. It was a waste of precious time and brain cells, yet it was a necessary evil that I couldn't stand.

"Shoot me the link," Jack said.

He didn't even need details. That was how much both of us trusted the other.

I did, and a few minutes later he whistled.

"*Hot* man. She yours?"

Heat pooled in my belly.

"Yeah," I confirmed.

She was.

I just had to pull my shit together, first.

***

Two hours later, Jack shot me the original poster as well as the original poster's address and photograph, and I found myself in front of a metal shop, idling on my bike, waiting for the motherfucker to come outside.

It didn't take long.

It was near lunch time, and the entire lot was emptying faster than a disturbed wasp's nest.

The man went to his own bike, straddled it, and I pounced.

One second I was on my bike, and the next I was eight spaces over, pulling the motherfucker off of his.

One well-placed fist to the man's nose had the little shit doubling. The next fist hit one of the man's kidneys.

"Pissing blood for a week," I heard someone mutter.

I knew they were there.

I could see about ten of them, but not one of them tried to interfere.

Either that meant they didn't like the guy I was about to teach a lesson, or they didn't want to be on the receiving end of my fists…or possibly both.

"Should we call the cops?"

They could always try, but likely the one to come was going to be Aaron since I'd warned him it may happen twenty minutes before.

"No."

That was the same voice that said the man would be pissing blood for a week, and I found that I kind of liked him.

Reaching down, I picked the man's head up by his hair, and turned him to look at me.

"You took a picture," I said angrily. "Do you know which one I'm talking about?"

The lower half of the man's face was covered with blood.

"No," he said.

Tears and snot were intermingling with the blood on his face, and I sneered at him in disgust.

"Let me remind you," I pulled out a photo I printed out and shoved it up against his face, letting the blood hit the paper and smearing it hard into his face.

He cried out.

"How about now?" I asked, pulling it back slightly. "Do you remember now?"

He started to fight back and I grinned, dropping the photo on the ground.

The man with the deep, amused voice behind me picked it up, and then cursed.

"You did this, Tyson?" the man asked.

Tyson, the douche that deserved way worse than an ass beating, threw out a punch that landed on my arm and grazed my bicep.

I retaliated by dropping my knee down onto the man's balls and grinding down.

I followed it up by kicking the man's knee, causing it to turn sideways—likely breaking his kneecap in the process.

He bellowed in pain, unsure what to hold—his balls, his nose, or his knee.

I stood up and started to back away, and he tried to follow.

So I dropped back down, the weight of my knee on his chest.

It was a miniscule try, but I had to give him credit. Most men would've been down and out by now.

"Stay the fuck down," I growled, leaning my knee into the man's sternum. "I ever, *ever*, see you share something this offensive again, I will rip your goddamn eyes out and shove them up your ass with the rest of your head."

The man nodded, licking his broken and cracked lips.

I stood, this time happy to see he wasn't going to try to follow.

Turning to my bike that was still running at the edge of the parking lot, I started towards it, uncaring that the men surrounding me watched me with wary looks.

"Truth?"

I looked up to see a bearded man holding the photo.

His beard was much larger than mine, and tied in a goddamned braid.

"What?" I half snapped.

"My name is William."

I shrugged.

His mouth twitched.

"I'm Randi's husband. Verity's best friend."

Understanding dawned.

I held my hand out as I said, "Nice to meet you."

He took my offered hand and shook it twice before letting go.

"I like what you did back there. Had I known, I'd have done it myself four days ago," he promised.

I shrugged.

"I just saw it this morning. Been dealing with funeral arrangements for my grandparents."

And waiting for my family to make it into town.

Not to mention finishing up a class session.

And avoiding anything that had to do with Verity.

Any sympathy on her part would cause me to break down, and right now I needed to be strong.

Because if I wasn't strong, I would cry like a goddamned baby.

"You ever need anything, a favor, I'm here."

I studied the man's face, noted his sincerity, and nodded once.

"Thanks."

With that, I mounted my bike—having gone back to the seatless one—and throttled it up as loud as it would go, sparing one final glance at the piece of shit still on the ground, before I rode away, back to my workshop and all of the problems that plagued me.

CHAPTER 8

Beards make my nipples have minds of their own.

-Verity's secret thoughts

Verity

"What are you doing?"

I looked up at my best friend, tears dripping down my face, and shook my head.

"Nothing," I said as I tried to wipe away my tears before she saw them.

She sighed, and took a seat next to me.

"Is it that man, or is it the meme again?" she asked.

I shook my head.

"Both."

And it was, but more of the sadness was directed toward Truth than my own fat ass at the moment.

"I still can't believe someone would put that on Facebook. You didn't even look bad! Seriously, it was you sitting on the back of a bike…though, I am fairly sure I could see the pink thong you bought at Victoria's Secret last week."

William started to chuckle darkly next to me, and I flipped him off, causing his smile to widen.

William and I had a weird relationship.

I started dating William first, and after a few weeks of dating, we both knew it wasn't going to work.

Then came in Randi.

I introduced her to him, and they really hit it off.

Flash forward six months, and they were engaged to be married. Now, six years later, they were married with five kids.

Literally, five kids.

And I wasn't sure that Randi was done yet.

William liked keeping her pregnant, and Randi liked making William happy.

It was vicious cycle, and one that would only end if one of them got their baby makers taken care of.

"So, I had a thing happen at work today," William started. "You'll never guess who got his ass kicked."

My heart leapt into my throat.

"Was it Tyson?"

Was that a hint of hope I heard in my voice? You bet your ass. I hated Tyson with a passion.

"Yep," he confirmed much to Randi's and my amusement. "Got his ass kicked thoroughly. By a big ass biker with a beard that has almost as much grandeur as mine."

I snorted, my hand going to my neck where Truth had given me a slight beard burn the last time I'd seen him…held him.

"Yep. Guy made sure that little fucker will be pissing blood for a week, thank God." He started to chuckle darkly. "The boss man told him to take a week off to get rid of his menstrual pains."

I rolled my eyes, but inside, deep down, I thought it was funny.

Tyson was a douche.

He'd never missed an opportunity to give me hell, and since he worked with Kenneth and William, I saw the little bastard at all the company functions.

Though, Kenneth was a big boss, the douche canoe who made sure everyone was doing their jobs correctly and thought he was better than all the grunts and peons at the company.

William was one of those peons, though not because of any lack of trying on the company's part in attempting to get him to take on more responsibilities. He just plain didn't want the job, and he liked it exactly where he was.

He made damn good money as a machinist, but he just didn't want the extra headache of having to deal with assholes like Tyson.

"That's the best news I've heard all day," I hesitated. "Do you...do y'all think I should go to the funeral?" I licked my dry lips. "I don't want him to think I'm stalking him, but I want to be there...just to show my face. Let him know I care."

Randi's face softened. "I think you should go."

"I don't know," I murmured.

William, Randi's husband, butted in then.

"I think you should go, too."

I blinked, startled to hear him offer an opinion.

"Why? What makes you think he won't see me and get mad?"

He grinned, causing his braided beard that was lying flat against his chest—something he did when he was about to ride—to shake, and gestured for me to sit up.

He sat down next to me, pulling me into his chest like a brother would—though I could only guess since I didn't actually have a brother—and started to talk.

By the time he was finished explaining the merits of going versus not going, I was convinced that he was right.

I should go.

"Now I just need to find something to wear."

That turned out a lot harder to do than making the actual decision to go in the first place.

CHAPTER 9

*If you're going to get in trouble for hitting
someone, you might as well hit them hard.*

-Fact of Life

Truth

My parents and my brother and sister made it in time. Even though we weren't quite sure if my sister would or not.

I suppose that was to be expected when you were in the middle of the ocean on an aircraft carrier, and it wasn't as easy to leave as someone who was on land could.

My brothers were at my back: Sean, Aaron, Big Papa, Ghost, and Tommy Tom.

The rest of the community—those who adored my Pops and Grams as much as I did—were also there.

Police officers. Paramedics. Firefighters. Plumbers. Even the fuckin' mayor was there.

The hall that we'd settled on to hold the service in was filled to maximum capacity, and my heart swelled knowing that the place was packed.

I heard a familiar voice say 'excuse me' from somewhere behind me, and I turned in my seat next to my mother, freezing at the sight that awaited me.

Verity, in a black dress that hugged her curves and came to a stop right above her calves, was taking a seat about four rows from the back, next to a few of my GG's bingo partners.

They smiled at her, scooted over, and made her feel welcome, causing my chest to ache.

I should've called her myself, but if I was being honest, I was using the death of my grandparents as an excuse. A convenient excuse that allowed me the time I needed to figure out what exactly I was going to tell her.

She looked up then, her eyes searching the room, and froze when she found me already looking at her.

She smiled and gave me a small wave.

I continued to stare, causing her eyebrows to furrow.

Then I lifted my hand and motioned my fingers at her, ordering her silently to come to me.

Her eyes widened, and she shook her head furiously.

The old ladies around her, though, saw that I wanted her, and all got up as one and ushered her out of her seat.

Not even five seconds later, Verity was on her feet in the middle of the aisle.

She was left standing there, looking at where she used to be sitting, wondering whether she should run for it or follow directions.

I leaned forward in my seat, then stood, gesturing to my mom to scoot down, which she did without another word.

"Verity," I said, my voice barely audible. "Sit."

She turned on her heel, and walked up to the pew I was standing in the middle of.

"'Scuse me," Verity said to my brother.

My brother stood, swiping his tie down against his chest as he did, and moved without a word.

Kenneth, who was on the end of the pew behind me, stood, and stared at Verity with a look of shock crossing over his face.

She looked damn good.

I agreed with his assessment.

What I did not agree with, however, was him reaching for her.

"Abel," I said quietly.

Abel, seeing that Kenneth was reaching for Verity, moved in front of Kenneth and blocked his way, allowing Verity to slip past him and my sister, Marnie, before coming to a stop beside me.

She smiled timidly at me, and I dropped my mouth down to hers, giving her a quick, soft kiss.

She had no clue, but she'd just saved my sanity.

Having to deal with my sister, brother, mother and father, as well as having Kenneth and my cheating ex at my back, was hard in and of itself.

But having to do that while also laying my grandfather and grandmother—people who had been like second parents to me—in the ground was tipping me over the edge of reason.

I didn't have any patience today, and I hadn't had much for the last five days since my grandparents had been murdered.

"I'm glad you're here," I told her, taking her hand, and pulling her to the pew beside me.

She crossed her left leg over her right and leaned into me.

"Are you okay?" she whispered in my ear.

I squeezed her to me, wrapping my arm around her shoulders, and held on tight.

My sister, who was curious by nature, stared at me over the top of Verity's head, and I winked at her.

She stuck her tongue out at me, and I felt something tight in my chest relax.

Marnie, Abel, and I had had a knockdown, drag out fight with our parents over the last two days about whether we should cremate my grandparents or not.

They agreed with our aunt, Kenneth and Eugene's mom, that they should be buried in a cemetery next to each other.

I'd argued that that hadn't been what the two of them wanted, and Abel and Marnie had agreed.

In the end, my parents finally settled with us, and we'd outvoted our aunt, but it hadn't been because they were agreeing with us. It'd been because the lawyer had butted in and informed my dad and aunt of their parents' wishes.

The music that'd been playing changed, and my body jerked at the realization that the service was about to start.

The funeral home had gone over everything that they were going to do, down to the last detail, and I knew the sound of my grandparents' wedding song signaled the beginning of the service.

My eyes went to the screen above the microphone, and my heart ached when I saw the first picture was of my grandfather and me fishing.

The next was of my sister, him, and my grandmother riding on a motorcycle, almost exactly like the one that had been plastered all over the Internet with a rude, derogatory comment right above Verity's ass.

As the pictures flowed through the slideshow, Verity leaned her head against my chest and rested her hand on my thigh, completely ignoring the angered eyes of Kenneth.

I turned my head slightly once to see him staring at Verity, and I turned back. Without flipping him off, might I add…though it was close.

As the slideshow came to a close, another song started to play, and I immediately stood, as did the men two pews back.

The National Anthem.

My grandfather had served twelve years in the Army while my grandmother had served eight. It'd been where they met.

My grandfather had come to my grandmother, a nurse, after a suspicious case of gout had nearly brought him to his knees.

And the rest was history.

They spent nearly every waking moment together from that point on and had even died on the same day.

Which, I guess, was a blessing.

I didn't see one lasting long without the other—especially knowing the other had died so brutally.

Verity's hand on my knee, circling it with one blunt fingertip, brought me back to the present, and I buried my fingers in her hair, wishing this thing would be over with already.

But it didn't happen fast.

It was the slowest funeral I'd ever been to, and I didn't know if that was due to the fact that there were actually two funerals happening at once, or if the people that spoke were just talking for irrationally long times.

Whatever the reason, by the time it all ended over an hour and ten minutes later, I was practically jumping out of my skin.

My body itched in this brand new, long sleeved dress shirt. I had a suit jacket on that restricted my movement, and the pair of pants I was wearing were one size too small.

Verity's presence, though, kept me comfortable, and she stayed with me the entire time.

By the time the funeral coordinator gestured for the family to leave, I was already on my feet and urging Verity to walk quickly—which she thankfully did after she got out of the pew.

My brother and sister followed suit, keeping up with my retreating back, and piled into the same car as me.

"Mom's going to kill us," Abel muttered, looking at the crowd that started to seep out of the auditorium's doors.

"Mom can suck it," I mumbled, leaning back into the seat and staring tiredly at the roof. Remembering my manners, though, I leaned forward and took Verity's hand. "Verity, this is my brother, Abel, and my sister, Marnie."

Marnie waved her fingers, and Abel gave her a nod.

"This is the girl that you were talking about?" Abel asked after a while.

I nodded and brought Verity's hand up to rest on my thigh as I stretched my own arm out behind her on the seat.

Bikes started up around the car we were in, and I relaxed even further.

"Are you going to be all right?" Verity asked softly. "You don't look too good."

"Big brother here doesn't like crowds," Marnie offered. "It took everything he had to be in that building with all of those people. That was thanks to our Aunt Eloise and our mom, though. If we'd have had our way, we would've had a wake like Pop and Grams wanted, instead of going through all this."

Verity blinked, then opened her mouth to say something.

However, nothing came out.

Instead she just shook her head and gestured to the bikes.

"What's up with the biker brigade?" she continued to ask questions.

"They're my club," I answered. "They're here for moral support."

Her mouth lifted up into a smile.

"Well, they're doing a damn fine job keeping everyone away from you."

I looked out the same window that Verity was, my mouth twitching when I saw the crowd heading our way.

However, Big Papa and Peek were holding them off with a scowl covering their faces.

"Peek loves him," Marnie whispered. "You're lucky they're here, big brother."

I was.

I was also lucky Verity was here.

I wouldn't have been able to get through the last hour and a half without her soothing touch calming me down.

Making me see reason.

That was until Kenneth shoved his way between Big Papa and Aaron, making his way to the car.

Peek gave the stupid man an annoyed look, but let him by when I waved him away.

"Here we go," Abel mumbled.

Verity turned her face into my arm, and I became irrationally annoyed at the fact that that man had the nerve to say a goddamned word to me, or even approach the same vehicle that I was in.

"What do you want?" I asked, rolling the window down just far enough to hear him and he could hear me.

"I wanted to make sure that Verity was…"

Verity's head popped up, and she glared. "I'm fine. Or I would have been had you left me alone. I'm here to offer Truth support on one of the hardest days of his life. So, if you don't mind, I'd like you to please leave."

I laughed and rolled the window up. Apparently, she didn't need me to fight her battles for her.

"I sense a story…" Marnie murmured. "And since we're stuck here until the cars move, why don't y'all tell us the story of how you met."

Verity's smile wasn't forced any longer.

"As long as Truth has no problem with me telling it…"

I shifted my fingers back into her hair, leaned my head back, and urged her on with a wave of my hand.

"After you."

***

Two hours later, my mother, father, sister and her good friend who'd driven down with her, as well as my brother, Verity, and I sat around the table, eating in silence.

Though, the rest of the men and women at the table, including the members of my club and their women, filled the silence around us—making the awkwardness of the past four days all but disappear.

Verity and I were at the end, and she was leaning into me as she listened to something Sean was telling the rest of the table.

My mother and father, finally deciding to join society, were listening to him talk about some patient he had, and I was thankful to finally have their attention off of me.

"What's going on with your parents?" she asked.

That was something I did not want to answer.

I hadn't spoken to my parents in over four years, and it wasn't because of lack of trying on my part.

It was due to the fact that they didn't like my life choices and had no problem letting me know it.

My brother and sister had been fairly neutral about the way I lived my life, but ultimately, they stayed out of it—which meant that they didn't choose sides, and saw all of us, just separately.

"My parents are upset that I chose to throw my life away to do a job that they didn't approve of," I finally settled on.

When I didn't expound, she chose not to pursue the topic, likely fearing I'd freak out and leave just like I'd done the last time we were together.

"I quit my job yesterday," she said into the silence. "I had a bad day, and my boss made a derogatory comment about a photo that's floating around the Internet of us…and I just snapped."

My stomach clenched. "I saw the photo," I murmured. "And I wasn't very happy about it."

She sighed.

"It's life," she finally settled on. "That's not to say that I wasn't extremely upset about it when I saw it."

I should really tell her that I found the guy who'd started the cruel photo circulating, but I didn't want to admit that I was the guy who caused the little shit-for-brains to be put into the hospital.

Instead, I blurted out what was on my mind, like usual.

"You wouldn't be willing to run a business, would you?" I teased her jokingly.

Her eyes widened.

"I would...if you needed me to. I've done it for years with my mom, and I've been in customer service for eight years now," she surprised me. "What would you need me to do?"

I thought about it for a second, and finally nodded, thinking it could work out great to have someone there I trusted.

"The pub already has a manager, kind of a service manager," I answered. "Really, I would just need you to be the person to make business decisions during the day when I can't be there, and be the boss man that everyone goes to with their petty problems. Like calling in sick, and complaining about customers...you know, stuff like that."

"What about payroll?" she asked, turning to face me.

"That's mine," I said. "I'll do that on Fridays before class starts, and if anyone has any problems with that, I'll take care of it Friday afternoon when I get out of class."

She nodded, her eyes distant as she thought about what I'd just offered her.

"I won't take anything over what I deserve," she finally said. "You can't pay me anything exorbitant."

My mouth twitched. "I'll pay you what I think you deserve."

Which was a lot, but she didn't need to know that.

"Well, okay," she settled into my side once again.

"So when are you opening the pub back up?"

That was my father, always asking the hard questions.

"I don't know," I admitted. "I was just discussing that with

Verity."

My father's eyes narrowed on the woman at my side.

"What does she have to do with when you're opening it?"

I clenched my teeth.

"Since I just asked her to be the fucking boss man," I snapped.

CHAPTER 10

*Have you ever been too nice, and ended up in a
situation which could've been avoided if you had
just been the asshole you were originally? Yeah,
me neither.*

-Truth's secret thoughts

Verity

I had a feeling I had just landed in the middle of a huge shitstorm,
and I could do nothing but sit still and wait it out.

I watched as father and son started throwing verbal slurs at each
other, and I realized something was really wrong with their
relationship. Fathers didn't say things like this to their kids. Not
now, and not ever, no matter what their age.

The entire table, all bikers, and siblings combined, all stared at
what was happening, too.

Truth's body, which had been pliant and almost relaxed only
moments before, was now stiff and vibrating with anger as he
pushed away from me.

"We're not doing this here and definitely not today of all days,"
Truth rumbled low in his throat.

His voice sounded nice and even, but his eyes told a completely different story.

"How's it feel to be dating a fucking killer?"

Those words were shot out of Truth's father's mouth, and I could do nothing but flinch at the anger that seethed inside of him.

"Ummm," I mumbled. "Maybe it's time for me to go?"

Truth's hand tightened on my hip, telling me without words that he wanted me to stay right the fuck there.

So I did, and I witnessed every single derogatory comment his father dished out.

And by the time he got to the fourth 'fucking waste of space and air,' I was done.

"Excuse me, Sir," I stood up and leaned forward. "I don't know who you think you are. I don't know why you think this is a good time to air out these old grievances, but it's not. It's inappropriate. First of all because we're in the middle of a restaurant, you're behaving badly and people are staring at you. Secondly, it's obvious that Truth is hurting. I can see it. You can see it. Hell, even the people in the kitchen washing the dishes can see it. So I suggest you either sit down and be quiet or leave."

Truth's father stood up like I'd poured ice cold water into his lap.

"Truth," he sneered, his breath wafting toward me. I could smell the alcohol all the way over here. "Don't you mean Ernest? Let me tell you something, Truth couldn't be a more hypocritical name for him. You don't know what he's done. You don't know who he's killed or why. I do, though. I watched him do it once."

My jaw clenched, and I picked up the first thing I could find, which happened to be a roll, and threw it at him.

It hit him on the cheekbone and bounced back onto the table, landing on the table next to a very amused Abel's plate. "Go.

Home."

One of the men to my left started to chuckle, but I didn't dare take my eyes off of the man.

"Didn't realize you let women fight your battles, Son." Truth's father backed away, taking a hold of his wife's arm. "Though I guess I shouldn't be surprised that you can't handle your business."

"I can handle my business," Truth said, leaning back into his chair. "It's just sexier when she does it for me."

His dad sneered, downed the rest of his wine and left, dragging his wife by the arm as he went.

"So…" Abel broke the silence after they'd left. "Who wants dessert?"

***

I turned at my door, smiling slightly when I saw my cat through the window, tangled in the blinds and likely about to pull them down again.

"You have a cat," Truth murmured.

He said 'cat' like it was something disgusting that he didn't want to get anywhere near.

"Yes," I confirmed. "Do you want to come in?"

"Where was the cat last time I was here?" he asked.

"Mr. Stiffy doesn't come out much," I admitted. "And when he does, it's only to eat or sit in the window and watch the birds."

Truth frowned. "I'm not ready to talk about my life yet."

Would he ever be?

I tilted my head. "You're a big boy, Truth," I said. "If you want to keep secrets—as long as they're not hurting our relationship—then keep them. In the meantime, I'd like you to come inside and watch the rest of the '*How To Get Away With Murder*' marathon we started watching the other day."

He stared at me for a few long moments, then nodded once, his shoulders stiff.

He had lines on his face and bags under his eyes that spoke of the stress he'd been under during the last week since he'd been here, and I wished I could smooth them away with my lips.

I wasn't sure he was in that kind of a mood, though.

He struck me as a suffer-in-silence kind of man.

I'd likely never know if he was hurting unless I witnessed him grimacing in pain or he received the injury while I was there to witness it.

Holding the door open for him to enter, he did, and walked straight into the kitchen where he got down two wine glasses, a bottle from where he'd seen me pull them down from last time, and poured wine to the brim in both glasses.

I didn't think it'd be a good idea to mention he'd just used half a bottle of four-hundred-dollar wine.

Instead, I walked down the long hallway that separated the bedrooms from the large living room, and headed to my room, which was at the very end of the hall.

My eyes stayed on the badly-in-need-of-repair wood floors as I walked.

The moment I flipped on the bedroom light, I saw Mr. Stiffy bound into the hallway past me, causing me to gasp.

"Jesus Christ, you little fucker," I growled, glaring at the empty hallway behind me.

"You all right?"

"Yes," I yelled back to the stubborn man. "Cat scared me, is all."

I walked into my bedroom and rid myself of the horrid dress that felt like it was strangling me and tossed it into the pile that I reserved for the things that needed to go to the dry cleaners…though, I wouldn't need that anymore.

Not when the only clothes that I got dry cleaned were the ones that I wore to work at the newspaper—a place where I no longer worked anymore.

I was standing there, contemplating whether it was acceptable to put on sweatpants, when I felt eyes on me.

I turned my head slowly, unsurprised to find him standing in the doorway to my room, staring at me.

"Yes?" I asked, reaching for the sweats.

He'd have to get used to them eventually.

When I wasn't working, I was in sweats, comfy shorts, or no pants at all.

I hated wearing real pants almost as much as I hated my old job.

He watched as I slipped my feet into my sweatpants, and continued to watch as I pulled down an old t-shirt that I'd cut up and made into a work out shirt.

The next thing I did was bend over and put my hair up into a messy bun, snagging the black hair tie that was on the floor next to my feet as I gathered all my hair on top of my head and stood up.

As I stood, I came face-to-chest with Truth and froze.

"What's wrong?" I whispered.

"I had one of the shittiest days of my life today," he swallowed thickly. "And then you defended me in front of my family and friends. I appreciate that more than you will ever know."

I smiled and leaned forward, wrapping my arms around his hips and hugging his big body to me.

My face laid flat against the leather of his biker vest, and I felt at peace for the first time since I'd read that meme and seen my ass hanging off the back of Truth's bike.

Though, I hadn't felt all that great before that with the way he'd left so abruptly.

But now, standing in the man's arms, I realized that none of that mattered right now.

Was I curious to know his secrets and motives behind doing what he'd done? Sure. Was I going to let that get in the way of what I knew was growing between us?

No way in hell.

"Let's go watch some TV."

He gave me one last long squeeze, and then let me go, taking my hand and leading me to the living room and my amazing couch where our glasses of wine sat.

Though, I noticed that he gave me the one he'd drank from already.

Not that I minded.

I just thought it was funny.

And as we watched season two of the show we'd started last week, I felt at home for the first time in a very long time.

CHAPTER 11

*Just because I'm a gentleman, doesn't mean that
I won't spank you.*

-Food for thought

Truth

I woke up to the feeling of light touches trailing over my face.

My eyes slowly snapped open, and I came face-to-face with Verity, who was staring at me like I was some interesting science project she was trying to figure out.

"You're awake?"

I nodded, a yawn stealing my breath as I moved my arms up high over my head and stretched my back and legs.

"Yeah," I said gruffly in between yawns. "What are you waking me up so early for?"

She pointed to the side table where my phone started to go off, and I sighed.

"Big Papa," I mumbled.

Reaching to the desk, I picked it up and answered it, listening to what Big Papa had to say.

"Is he dead?" I asked the moment he told me why he was calling.

"We found him in an alley right outside the pub," Big Papa answered. "Not dead…yet. But he will be soon, if all the blood loss was any indication."

I cursed.

"You get anything out of him?"

I crossed my fingers like a child but was disappointed.

"His throat was sliced when we got to him," Big Papa answered. "It was obvious that we were meant to find him before he was dead. There was a note pinned to the body with a fucking knife dedicating the kill to you. The anonymous 911 caller also called and told us exactly where to find him."

"Did you trace the call?"

"Yes," Big Papa snorted. "Was traced back to a pay phone outside the pub."

I grunted.

"What else is there?"

He didn't pretend to hold anything back, but that was also because I was a knowledgeable source of information, as well as a good resource. I'd been an instructor for going on eight years now at the police academy, and I'd been a resource utilized by TPD for six of them.

"The academy was vandalized," he answered. "Nothing too bad, but there's graffiti, as well as damage to the outside gates and cruisers."

"You think it's related?" I assumed.

"Yes," he answered. "But not because there's any evidence that there is, it's just a gut instinct."

"Did you tap into the video surveillance?"

"Yes," he sighed. "Nothing at all. Every single camera angle from both the store where he was found and at the academy was clean. Not one single person was caught on it."

I growled in frustration.

Of course they were able to avoid them.

That spoke of professionalism, not petty crime to me.

It didn't matter, though. I knew exactly who it was that left that particular calling card.

Elais fucking *Beckett.*

"Why do you say they're connected?" I feigned confusion.

The less people that knew this man was in town, the better.

"Nothing concrete, just a feeling," he answered. "I just wanted to give you a head's up, anyway. Didn't want to surprise you."

You did enough, I thought morosely. *Just knowing that man is in the same town as me is enough to set my hair on end...and that's quite a feat seeing as I don't have much in the way of fucking hair.*

Beckett's fault again.

Six years ago, when I got out of the Navy, I'd hooked up with a black ops group that was—or so I thought at the time—in the business of rescuing and recovering children who were kidnapped and being held hostage all over the world.

What it actually turned out to be, though, was my inability to see anything bad in an old man who looked and acted like my grandfather. The same fucking man that my grandfather had introduced me to and who had been like a second grandfather to me for the entirety of my life.

The same man that my father warned me about when I first started working for him.

I'd trusted my grandfather, though, and it'd been the one and only time he was ever wrong. But, Jesus Christ, was it a doozy.

Why? Because I'd killed a man. Although that man hadn't been innocent by any stretch of the imagination, he did have the right to be tried for his crimes in the United States, and I'd robbed him of that right.

Five minutes later, I hung up the phone, letting it drop down onto the bed at my side.

"You okay?" She pressed a kiss to my pec, right above my nipple, and my dick stirred.

I was a sick mother fucker.

Not even ten minutes ago, Big Papa had told me the gruesome details of a man's death, and now I was hard.

Not to mention that there was a man here in the city who would like nothing more than to see me dead just like my grandparents.

The same man who was sent to prison because of me—and whose release I apparently had not been told about.

But did that stop my dick from getting hard as she trailed kisses down my sternum?

Fuck no.

Yeah, definitely going to hell.

As I rolled over and pinned her underneath my body, I delighted in the gasp that left her throat. And I didn't let the outside world—nor my conscience—intervene for the next thirty minutes as I made it my mission to forget anything and everything while in turn I memorized Verity's body.

"Baby," I rasped against her neck, widening her thighs with my knees and pushing her legs farther apart.

"What?" she breathed, her lips turning to fan over the line of my jaw.

My beard rasped against those soft lips, and she moaned.

My hands moved from her breasts to her arms, sliding up over soft skin until I had a delicate wrist in each hand.

Pinning them to the bed above her head, I dropped my mouth, running it over the length of her neck and then even further along the top of her collarbone.

"Jesus," she rasped. "You make me act like I've never done it before."

A blush of red stole up her chest, infusing her cheeks, and I grinned.

She was fucking adorable.

I chuckled and dropped my head down, catching one stiff nipple between my lips and biting down gently.

Her whole body bowed off the bed, and her naked bottom half arched up, seeking the touch of my cock against her softness.

I gave her what she wanted, grinding down my hard cock into the warmth of her sex.

Her heat practically scalded me where we touched, and I closed my eyes and moaned around the tip of her breast.

Her fingers curled into fists as her back came off the bed, pushing more of her full breasts into my mouth.

I opened wider to take it and then sucked hard.

Over and over again, I licked, sucked, tugged and nibbled on her nipple, lavishing it with the attention it deserved.

Releasing her wrists to use my hands to cup her breasts, I switched my mouth to the other nipple and gave it the same treatment.

She dug her heels into the bed, thrusting her hips up and forcing my cock to grind even harder into her pussy.

"Please," she moaned. "I need you."

I knew exactly what she meant.

My cock was swollen and throbbing, and if I didn't get inside of her soon, I was fairly sure I would die from lack of blood to my brain.

She reached down when I wasn't fast enough to obey her orders, and gave me two pumps with her smooth, soft hand before placing the tip of my cock against her entrance.

I grinned at her, and slowly let my hips drop.

The minute her heat engulfed the swollen head of my cock, I shuddered from the pleasure of it.

I sank all the way inside her to the base of my shaft. I knew that whatever I did, this was right.

She was right.

Everything about her was right.

I moaned into her neck as she took all of me, latching my hands onto her hips with a strong grip.

My fingers dug into the meat of her ass, and my thumb pressed down against her hip bone, causing her own feminine growl to escape.

"You feel so fucking good, baby. Like a dream," I rasped, sweeping my lips up the line of her jaw.

She pulled at my beard, causing me to look up into her eyes.

"You're the best I've ever had and I don't want you to ever stop," she whispered fiercely.

I grinned against her lips, and then pressed down, letting my tongue trail against her bottom lip before replying.

"I gotta go to work some time, sweet girl," I murmured. "And I'm fairly sure you said you'd help me with the pub."

She sighed, her breath fanning out against my lips, and I chuckled.

"I guess you're right," she murmured. "But I'm ready and willing anytime you want to take me."

I growled, then pulled my hips back and snapped them forward.

The loud slap-slap filled the room around us as I continued to fuck her with long and hard thrusts.

She started coming on the fourth stroke, and didn't stop until I pulled back and waited for her pussy to release the stranglehold she had on my cock.

I didn't want to blow yet. I wanted to enjoy this for a little bit longer before reality intruded once again.

Which I showed her as I took her for a very long time afterward.

By the time she was a writhing mass of stray hairs and sweaty body parts underneath me, my balls were screaming for release.

"One more," I ordered.

She shook her head, the long brown strands seeming to stick absolutely everywhere.

My chest. Her chest. My neck, her armpit.

Hell, a lot of it was even underneath her back and causing her neck to arch, giving me perfect access to run my beard over the sensitive skin there which seemed to really drive her wild.

"One more," I repeated, pulling out of her completely and dropping down between her legs until her feet rested on my shoulders.

The first swipe of my tongue against her clit had her moaning in denial. "Nooooo," she whimpered. "I can't."

The next swipe—a sweet burst of flavor that was all Verity—had her rolling over to her belly to flee.

I caught her around the ankles and yanked her down until she was over the side of the bed.

Her feet didn't touch, and that was okay with me.

The less purchase she had, the less chance she had of getting away from me.

Placing both of my hands on her ass cheeks, I parted them and bent forward, resuming my attack.

She cried out, and then tensed when I swirled one blunt finger around her entrance.

"God," she breathed. "You're sadistic."

I let my beard trail up the inside of her thighs and she shivered as goosebumps broke out over her skin.

"I can do it…please. Just get inside of me."

I knew she could, but I was going to taste this one before I released inside of her.

And she knew it, too, as she turned her head to the side and watched me lick her through the mirror over her dresser.

I penetrated her with a third finger, I sucked harder on her clit, and that was all it took.

She tried to get her knees under her to pull away, but I held her tight with my shoulders, pinning her to the bed as I continued to my oral assault on her pussy.

Once she was finished contracting around my fingers, she was breathing hard, and I was nearly bursting.

Standing, I straddled her backside.

It took two rough strokes of my cock over tight ass before I was coming, the juices of her pussy lubing my hand as I jerked off.

White splashes of cum landed on her back and ass, and by the time I was falling over to the bed beside her, I was heaving out my breaths right along with her.

I was sweaty, hot, and sated.

And I wanted nothing more than to lie here and do that a hundred times over again.

"That was the hottest, best sex I've ever experienced in my life, and I think I need a smoke and a drink now," she mumbled into the mattress.

She lay still, not quite able to move yet, and I liked the sight of my release decorating her back, so I stayed right where I was, too, gathering my wits and staring at the beautiful woman beside me.

"I need a towel," came her muffled reply.

I snorted and got out of bed, snatching my underwear off the floor, and my pants off the bed post, before heading to the bathroom.

Pulling on my underwear, followed by my pants, I left them zipped but unbuttoned and then grabbed the rag off of the towel holder and wet it down.

Wringing it out, I walked back into the bedroom only to find her in the same position, face down on the bed.

"You okay over there?" I asked her, placing the wet rag against her back and methodically cleaning my release from her.

She squeaked when the cool towel hit her skin, and goosebumps broke out over her back, arms, and legs.

A tease of sorrow hit me as I cleaned the last remnants of my release off completely, and I tossed the rag a little harder than I should have, beaming the wall across the room with it before it fell into the hamper underneath.

"I better not have jizz on my walls," she muttered, turning her head.

I smiled and dropped a kiss to her cheek before getting up and searching for my t-shirt.

"Have you seen my tee?" I asked. "I have to be at a class in about thirty minutes."

"The last time I saw it, it was out in the living room," she muttered, eyes closing once again in the early morning sunlight that was streaming through her partially open blinds.

I buttoned my pants and hooked my belt as I made my way to the living room, spotting my fucking tee exactly where she said it was, but annoyed to find the goddamned cat sitting on it, cleaning its ass.

"Get off, fucker," I muttered, yanking it out from underneath him.

The cat lithely got to his feet, tossed me a hiss, and then walked off with his tail twitching in the air.

I curled my lip and shook out my shirt before I shrugged it on.

Immediately, I sneezed.

I was allergic to cats…had I mentioned that?

Not so allergic that I couldn't be in the same house with them, but allergic enough that if they slept on my goddamned shirt, I would be sneezing and likely itching until I could get a shower.

I'd just turned the corner to head back to her room when I stopped in my tracks.

She was standing there, leaning against the wall, waiting for me.

"You don't like my cat?" she guessed.

I snorted.

"No," I murmured. "But only because I'm allergic to them."

Her eyes widened.

I sneezed again.

"I…don't know what to do," she finally admitted.

I winked at her.

"It's okay. I'll go home, take a shower, and everything will be back to normal…promise."

She pursed her lips.

"Trust me." I held up my hands, one in the air, and one out flat, like I was swearing on a bible.

Then the words she said next stopped me in my tracks.

"I trust you completely, Truth. With my heart and with my body," she whispered. "You're a good man."

I wasn't a good man.

The words my father hurled at me as he'd left dinner stuck with me.

She had to be curious. That had to also be the root of why she was saying this to me in the first place. She wanted to reassure me that she was on my side…and she shouldn't be.

And as I left five minutes later after getting one final goodbye kiss, I knew that I needed to leave. If Elais Beckett found out about Verity, he wouldn't lose a wink of sleep in his quest to make sure that Verity endured the same fate as my grandparents.

He'd made me a promise five years ago—one that I thought he'd never be able to carry out—that he would make my life a living hell.

Too bad I didn't believe him.

It might've saved me a whole lot of heartache.

CHAPTER 12

I either give too many fucks or not enough fucks.
It's like I can't find a middle ground for perfect
fuck distribution.

-Verity's secret thoughts

Verity

I was at work, but he wasn't.

At least he'd told the crew that I was now in charge. If he hadn't, I would've left. None of them trusted me at this point, anyway. I'm just a woman that the new boss man was banging, and they thought I got this job because I was fucking him.

Which couldn't be further from the truth...*could it?*

Normally, I wouldn't doubt myself. Not even a little bit.

However, it'd been five days—which seemed to be a common occurrence with him—since I'd seen him, and I was beginning to wonder what in the hell I was thinking working this job.

Though, that didn't stop his brother and sister from coming in two days ago telling me goodbye, and giving me hugs.

It was the sympathy I saw in their eyes that had me biting my lip and trying to figure out what in the hell was going on.

Was there more to what his father said than I knew?

And if so, was he ever going to tell me about it?

As I walked out of the pub around two p.m., confident that the crew could handle the rest of the afternoon and dinner crowd, I knew I was going to light into him the next time I saw him.

What gave him the right to string me along like this?

Getting into my car, I drove to Truth's place first, then to the police station.

I didn't know why I went there. I didn't really know anybody on the force except Big Papa. I knew for a fact that he'd talk to me.

He may not tell me where Truth was, but he'd tell me if he was okay…which at this point was what I really needed.

Confident in what I was about to do, I pulled into a spot next to a police car and turned off my own car, staring at the big brown building with a look of foreboding.

This likely wasn't a good idea.

Truth knew people in there, and I didn't want to embarrass him.

But I was concerned, and a little bit mad.

I wanted answers, and I wanted them now.

As I got out of the car, I was determined to get my answers.

I had my bad ass face on, and as I marched into the police station, head held high, I headed toward the first officer I could find and demanded to see Big Papa.

"BP is in a meeting."

My sails deflated.

"What about Aaron?"

The hard-nosed woman sneered. "I can help you."

I rolled my eyes.

"No offense, ma'am, but I'm looking for someone, either Aaron or Big Papa. You aren't a substitute for them," I admitted.

I could tell I'd offended her.

Her badge said Stephanie, and just when I was about to offer an apology, Aaron appeared around a corner, his phone to his ear.

He saw me immediately, and his eyes narrowed.

Coming straight to me, he latched onto my elbow and started to pull me in the direction he wanted me to go.

Which, apparently, was outside and around the building.

All the while he maintained his conversation he was having on the phone.

"Yes, Sir," he said. "I'll talk to my wife about it, and after we discuss it, I'll get back to you. Tomorrow morning, afternoon at the latest."

We'd just rounded the corner when Aaron's K-9 partner appeared, startling the ever-loving shit out of me.

"Sorry," he said as he pocketed the phone. "Tank likes to stay outside when Stephanie is in the vicinity."

I snorted.

"I believe I offended her," I admitted.

Aaron didn't even try to deny it. "You probably did, but she gets offended easily. And nobody likes her, so I don't really care."

I blinked.

"Okay," I finally settled on. "What's up with that, though? And where are you taking me?"

He was leading me down the side of the building toward the

woods.

I didn't know the man all that well, either. Maybe he was going to take me to the woods and put me out of my misery. Maybe he was going to lead me to some super-secret camp where all the recruits went to learn Batman stuff that they would be able to utilize while on the job as a police officer.

Hell, maybe I just had a good imagination.

Whatever the reason, I wasn't expecting to find anyone in the woods. I was expecting to be led to my doom…or something.

So when I saw Truth, decked out in black tactical pants, black boots that laced up all the way to mid-calf, a skin tight black t-shirt with Mooresville Police emblazoned in white vinyl on his back, and a black cap with MPD stitched on it, I froze.

Literally froze.

Stopped right in the middle of the trail, causing Aaron to stop and turn.

"What?" he asked, worried that I'd seen something disturbing on the ground.

I waved him away.

"Nothing," I licked my lips. "Does he always dress like that?"

Aaron's gaze shifted from the ground to where I was staring, and he snorted.

"You women are always the same. The man's working. His clothing choice is purely functional, not fashionable."

I shrugged.

"You…"

"What are you doing here?"

I froze, looking away from Aaron to see Truth twisted and looking at me from about ten paces away.

"I'm looking for you," I admitted. "Do you have a minute?"

He didn't even hesitate to answer.

"No."

I blinked.

"You…what?" I was confused. "Are you sure you can't spare me just a few…"

"Go home."

I blinked.

"But…"

"Go. Home," he ground out. "Aaron, escort her to her car."

"Wait, Truth," I held up one finger, trying not to stare at the pitying faces of the men and women standing behind Truth.

"Go *home*."

I ground my teeth together.

"I will not go home," I snapped.

"I'll come over later," he said once he realized I wouldn't budge.

I stared at him for a long time before I nodded. "Promise?"

He gave one quick nod. "Yes."

I crossed my arms over my chest, took one last look at the men and women staring at me, and then started back across the parking lot toward my car.

I got in, but I knew in my heart that he'd just lied to me.

He wouldn't be coming to see me later, and I was pissed off and hurt that he'd blatantly lied to my face.

But I knew one thing for certain. He wasn't getting off that easily.

I'd be going to his house tonight, whether he wanted me to or not.

***

I waited until nine that night before my impatience could no longer keep me in my home.

The drive to Truth's place was short, and it gave me practically zero time to prepare what I was going to say.

I'd been trying to compose a few words to tell him, but each and every time I came up with something, I dismissed it because it made me sound like a whiney child.

But now, whiney child sounding or not, I was going to make the man listen to me.

And he was going to listen to every single word I had to say, or I'd make him.

At least, I was going to until I walked into his house and found him drinking straight from a half empty whiskey bottle.

He was sitting on his couch, bottle dangling from two fingers over the arm, his head leaned back staring at the ceiling.

"I told you to go away."

"How do you know it's me?" I challenged him.

"Because your car sounds like a fucking bus that's ready to kick the bucket. It backfires as it shuts off, which is another distinctive tip off," he mumbled darkly, not bothering to make eye contact with me.

My car was bad. That'd been why Kenneth was buying me a new one, because it was in need of something more than I could offer it.

I could, I supposed, buy myself a new one. But I had a sentimental attachment to the old girl. She'd been the one constant thing in my life all the way through my high school years. She'd been my safe haven.

After Kenneth cheated, though, I couldn't find it in myself to look for a new car. So I stuck with the same old piece of shit that I'd been driving for years.

I closed the door behind myself and walked further into the room, wondering idly when the last time he cleaned up after himself was.

Shit was everywhere. Clothes. Shoes. Boots. Guns. Ammo. If Truth had used it at some point in the last two weeks since I'd been there, it was laying out where he happened to put it down.

It hadn't been cleaned since the last time I was there.

"The doctor told me to start drinking more," he told me, bringing my attention back to the pitiful state he was drinking himself into.

Tommy, the doctor of the club he was a member of, would not do that…especially with everything that'd happened to Truth over the last few weeks.

"I think he meant water, Truth," I offered darkly. "Not whiskey."

He shrugged.

"Semantics," he rumbled, then pulled the bottle up to his lips and took another swig.

I gritted my teeth.

"I was a bad guy once," he murmured into the darkness. "What my father says is true, but I'm not that man anymore."

I froze where I was standing.

"Would you like to tell me about it?"

He laughed humorlessly.

"No," he admitted. "But since you won't go away, I guess I'll have to share my sins with you."

I walked slowly forward and took a seat on the opposite arm of the couch that he was leaning against, and waited.

He started slowly.

Then picked up speed until he spilled every single one of his sins.

"When I got hurt two weeks into my final deployment, they medically discharged me."

"What happened? How did you get hurt?" I interrupted, suddenly concerned and unable to hide it.

His head rolled on the back of the couch, and he smiled in my direction.

"I burned my retina during a firefight and couldn't see down the barrel of my gun for about three months," he told me. "It was severe enough at the time to discharge me."

I nodded my head.

"Okay," I said, making a 'go ahead' motion with my hand. "What happened then?"

I felt like a freakin' shrink with the way I was urging him to move forward.

"I couldn't settle into civilian life, so my grandfather suggested that I go work for his best friend. He ran a rescue and recovery black ops organization, and I thought he was one of the good guys, in it for the right reasons." He swallowed. "Turns out, I was wrong. He was only in it to make a buck, a whole lot of bucks, actually. He had his own agenda that he didn't share with the rest of us grunts unless or until he felt like sharing it."

I didn't reply, waiting for him to continue. And he did.

Bitterly.

"One day, I was sent on a mission by Elais Beckett, the owner of the company and my grandfather's friend, and it all went well.

Intel was good. We found the kid. It was great, right up until it wasn't." He took another drink of his whiskey. "We were seconds away from making the recovery when the man came in, took hold of his son, and put a gun to his head."

My stomach dropped.

"Then what?" I pushed.

I wasn't sure whether I should urge him to continue talking or not, so I just did what I thought was best. Which was encourage, but not interrupt.

"Then I shot him. Shot right over that kid's head. My bullet entered the man's left eye, and expanded like it was supposed to do, which caused his brain to scramble and the bullet to leave out his left ear. Brains exploded, all over his son's face and body," he swallowed.

"I don't see why that was bad," I finally said. "I can see why it was 'bad' but not bad, bad. I mean, he was holding a gun to the child's head, right?"

He nodded. "Right. But what I didn't find out until moments later was that the gun the guy was holding was a plastic Airsoft gun, and it still had that stupid orange cap on the end of the barrel."

I hummed in understanding.

"The guy was fucking crazy," he said. "Probably would've killed the kid, but had I been paying better attention, we could've apprehended him and taken him in to get treatment, and that kid wouldn't have had his father's brain explode all over his face."

I bit my lip. "I'm still not seeing why that's so bad."

His eyes broke from mine.

"I did research on that kid. Found out later on that the father had signs of PTSD, and reacted badly when startled. Which I'd done. Had I not entered the building like I was ready to storm the place, he would've likely answered the door just like any other normal human being." I watched him swallow. "The mother, from reports I'd later read, had called it in not as an 'emergency' but as an 'I want him back, get him here' kind of call. Which Elais Becket had neglected to tell me about."

My stomach was sick for him.

"What about the 'killer' part that your father was tossing at you?"

"I did research on the other ops we'd done, and apparently that one case wasn't so isolated. I'd performed four ops that went sour. Four people were mentally impaired, sick, but generally good people." I was sick to my stomach. "Two of them died. Two of them are paralyzed. I killed them, and didn't even have any reason to, because they weren't bad guys. They were just lost. Like I'd been at one point."

He scratched his head with the lip of the whiskey bottle, and then leaned forward abruptly.

"And why does your dad call you a killer?" I asked, confused.

"Because I am."

"How does he know that you are?"

"Because I told him. One day I needed to unload, and he was convenient. But, he didn't make me feel better…only worse." He cleared his throat. "My words, and actions ruined our relationship, and I'll never have that back."

I felt terrible for him.

"What happened next?"

"I hunted Elais Beckett down," he said. "Hooked up with a man named Raphael that I knew from my SEAL days. He pulled some strings, and we got Beckett charged, tried and sent to prison after catching him red-handed pocketing ransom money from a rescue and recovery op that I actually think he orchestrated in the first place."

Okay...

"Truth…"

He held up his hand. "Let me finish."

I fell silent and waited for him to continue, which took a very long time.

"Elais Beckett made a vow to me the day I went to visit him in prison," he moaned and leaned forward, letting his head hang. "Should've fucking known that he'd get out. He should've been denied parole. He was the last two times he came up for release. Unfortunately, the only crime he was charged with was racketeering, and he got twelve years for it. He's served six of it, and the parole board obviously thought that was enough this time and let him go. Something that the detectives on his case failed to mention to me."

I frowned. "They don't normally 'forget' to do that, do they?"

His head came up.

"No."

The way he said it made my gut clench.

"What happened to them?"

"Dead." He looked me straight in the eyes. "Just like my grandparents."

Nausea boiled in my belly.

"He killed your grandparents."

One nod.

"And you think he's going to come after you, next," I assumed.

Another nod.

Another swig of the whiskey.

"And getting drunk is going to help you fend him off if he is coming?"

His jaw clenched, and he scratched the back of his neck.

"I'm a depressed mother fucker. Give me a goddamned break," he snapped, eyes flaring hotly with anger.

I held up my hands and stood from the arm of the couch.

The first thing I did was clear the table of the empty beer bottles and trash from his food over the past week.

"Gross," I said, holding up a piece of stale pizza.

He shrugged.

"I'm out of trash bags."

He was. I found that out almost immediately.

He did, however, have eight million, three hundred, and forty-seven Wal-Mart sacks stuffed into an old Dr. Pepper twenty-four pack box, so I started filling them up with the trash I could find around the house.

I didn't stop until I had eighteen bags filled.

"Jesus Christ, you're a slob," I told him, indicating the pile.

He set the bottle down with a clank, and stood.

His impressive height towered over me, but I wouldn't be intimidated.

Not this time. *Not with this man.*

"You need to get the fuck out of my house," he snapped. "Now, before I make you get out."

I knew for a fact he wasn't going to make me do anything. He wasn't that type of man.

But he would say stuff to purposely hurt me to get me to leave. And I had to keep him from doing that right then, so I shut him up with my mouth.

One second I was standing in front of him, and the next I launched myself at him.

He was either going to drop me or catch me.

Thankfully, he chose to catch me.

I was glad he did because otherwise I would've hit the floor hard with how high I'd jumped.

He grunted as my body hit his.

Curving his arm underneath my ass, he pulled me close to him, and slammed his mouth down onto mine.

One deep, long, wet kiss that showed both of our frustration over the situation.

His anger paired with my annoyance was enough to shoot that kiss to the next level.

I'd never, not ever, had angry sex before, but the second Truth shoved his hand up under my dress (yes, I'd planned this out incredibly well) and ripped my panties free from my body, I knew I was about to experience what angry sex was all about.

And I was right.

It was better than anything I'd ever experienced before in my life.

Emotions were heightened, making everything more forceful, more powerful, full of more feelings, just more *everything*.

His hand under my dress immediately honed in on where I was wet for him, and he teased my clit once before circling his large finger around my entrance.

"You should leave," he grated out.

I grabbed a hold of his beard roughly and pulled his mouth back down to mine.

Tomorrow I would have a beard burn.

Tomorrow I'd be sore.

Tomorrow I would deal with that, but right now I just didn't give a damn.

Truth was mine, and I was his, and there wasn't anything he could do about it.

I wasn't letting anybody, not even him, come in between us.

And as his fingers roughly entered me, I gasped into his mouth.

His head then dropped down and his teeth clenched the top of my dress and I heard a slight tearing sound. I didn't even care.

His mouth encircled my bare breasts (yes, I told you I planned well—no bra equaled easier access), and my mind was on only one thing.

Getting him inside of me. Something in which he gave me seconds later.

Still holding me, he moved us to the wall, pinning me to it with his big body, as he roughly ripped his sweatpants down and pulled out his big, fat cock, slamming it inside of me.

If I wasn't already soaking for him, he would've hurt me.

But I was ready and had been since I'd walked in the door, despite his terrible words.

One second I was yearning for him, and the next I was so full of him that I could barely breathe.

He didn't wait for me to catch my breath, either. One second he was seated fully inside of me, filling me to the brim, and the next he was fucking me.

Angrily. Aggressively.

My head slammed back against the wall, and I gasped as he fucked into me almost brutally. Hard, deep, unrelenting thrusts that bottomed out inside of me with each stroke letting me know that I would be tender tomorrow.

I didn't care.

Not one single bit.

Because that twinge of pain amped this up to the most pleasure I'd ever felt in my life.

His pubic bone was rasping over my clit with each thrust, and his hands on my hips, holding me in place, gripping just tightly enough to cause a little bit of discomfort, had me on the verge of coming unglued.

And just when I was seconds from coming, he pulled out of me so abruptly that I cried out.

"No!" I exclaimed.

But he wasn't done.

He carried me to his bed where he tossed me down unceremoniously.

I hit the bed, then gasped as he took me by my hips, flipped me to my knees, pulled me up high, and filled me again so fast that I tried to get away from the overwhelming sensations I was feeling.

He wouldn't let me, though.

He held my hips still, and continued to fill me over and over again. Roughly. Urgently.

Then his thumb brushed over my back entrance. Once, twice, three times before pressing inside.

I came before I even realized I was close again.

An explosion of light, the sound of my heart beating rapidly in my ears, coupled with all of the other things I was feeling collided and detonated inside me, taking me out in the most incredible, otherworldly orgasm of my life.

My knees went out from under me, and Truth followed me down, hips bucking as his big body shuddered.

I felt the rasp of his beard and the heaving of his chest against my back as I slowly came back to reality.

I was wondering if I was actually dead. If I wasn't, I knew for sure that I wouldn't be able to move for a few long seconds, and I wasn't sure I wanted to anyway.

Truth's body still blanketed mine, and it was heavy.

Really heavy.

But I liked it and I wanted to stay like this forever.

Or at least I had until Truth opened his mouth and ruined it all.

"It's time for you to go," he said, rolling over onto his back, not even bothering to warn me that he was pulling out of me so I could catch the lovely deposit he'd made in my vagina.

The man was a goddamned beast. It would be no surprise to learn that his swimmers were just as virile as he was.

"No."

"Yes," he said. "You're a good lay, Verity. You're a nice woman. But you need to leave. There's nothing here for us. Nothing that I even want. I only kept Destiny because she was a convenient fuck, but ultimately she left me the fuck alone and let me do what I wanted to do…you, well you're not like that. You'll bug the fuck out of me until I go crazy, and I just don't want that in a relationship. Because eventually, I'd just come to resent you for it. Besides, I'm not sure you're what I want in my life. Sorry."

I knew he was going to say words that were going to hurt me, but what I didn't expect was that he was going to say damn near the same ones that Kenneth had said to me. Something that I'd never told him about, so he didn't know how much they'd hurt me.

Maybe I was a nagger. Maybe I had a way of annoying men that turned them off.

Was it so bad that I cared about them? That I wanted what was best for them?

No. At least I didn't think so.

But maybe he was right. Maybe what we had wouldn't be the best thing for him. Or for me.

Shit. That's when I got pissed and used anger to cover up my pain.

"Funny thing, Ernest," I sneered. "You're much more like your cousin, Kenneth, than you know. Seems he had the same damn opinion of me." I said as I got out of bed.

I picked up the dress, which was slightly ruined but it would be okay enough to get me home, and slipped it on over my head.

Truth didn't even watch me.

His eyes were closed as he seemingly fell asleep, satisfied and sated.

At least that made one of us, I thought morosely.

CHAPTER 13

You're rubber, I'm glue. Eat shit and fuck you.

-Verity's very adult thoughts

Verity

I quit working at the pub.

I just didn't show up.

I hoped that all the work I'd put in didn't totally implode, but I suppose that wasn't my problem anymore.

At least it hadn't been until I opened the folder in a moment of weakness.

I'd had the folder since the night that I'd spent with Truth in Vegas.

I didn't know why I kept it. It was only some of the hotel information that I'd hastily grabbed as we'd left that day.

But it'd held sentimental value...or at least it had until now.

The first piece of paper I pulled out was a hotel receipt for room service.

The second was a receipt for flowers.

My brows furrowed.

"Flowers?" I mumbled, flipping to the next page.

And that's when my breath caught.

Because what I thought was just some hotel flyer, wasn't.

It was a cream piece of cardstock paper with gold embellishments on the side, shining and bright to bring attention to the words between the border.

And the words, yeah, those were shockers.

CERTIFICATE OF MARRIAGE

This certificate certifies that

Ernest Alan Reacher and Verity Ruthann Cassidy

Were united in marriage on this day

The third day of July two thousand sixteen.

The ceremony was officiated and witnessed

by Johnathan Roy Presley and Jezebell Reanald Corriander.

My stomach churned.

What had we done?

I did the only thing I could do.

I went to my GG, marriage certificate in hand, and cried onto her shoulder.

***

"I'm scared," I whispered to my grandmother.

My GG looked over at me, her face softened.

"If I could have anything in this world back right now, it would be your grandfather," she murmured softly.

My heart constricted.

"I know," I whispered. "I wish for him to be back all the time."

Her smile was soft and reassuring, but I could also see the sadness in her eyes.

"I think about him every night as I get ready for bed. I think about him when I close my eyes." She took a shaky breath. "But in my dreams, he's right back where he belongs. At my side." Her mouth pinched. "I knew that Kenneth wasn't for you, but you were happy, so who was I to say that he wasn't for you?"

I didn't reply.

"Does he take your breath away?"

I knew we were no longer talking about Kenneth, but about Truth.

"Yes," I said simply.

"What about when you're sleeping?" she asked. "Can you sleep without him?"

I thought about the night before, how I'd laid in bed for hours and hours just willing myself to finally go to sleep, only to let my mind wander to where it ultimately wanted to go. Him.

And then I'd be lost all over again.

"No," I finally admitted.

"The true test is," she stood up and walked to a picture of my grandfather and her that was hanging on the wall next to the kitchen sink. It was an older one, one that was taken two days before they got married forty-seven years ago. "Can you imagine your life without him? Does it hurt to think about him not being there anymore?" her voice cracked. "Can you see yourself going on a trip without him? Can you think about buying a car without his input? What about choosing paint color? When you think about what color you're painting the living room, can you imagine doing it without first getting his input? Because," she smiled, "if you can't, then you're already gone. If you think about him more than you think about anything else, you've already made the decision. Now stop putzing around and go get your man."

I stood up.

"But…his background."

My GG stared at me.

"I would've stood by your grandfather if he'd done those things …and I wouldn't have questioned him. He would have been mine, and that was the only question I ever needed answered." She hesitated. "What you've told me about your man, is that he really does care for you. He's made some bad decisions, yes, but he hasn't done anything so sinful that he won't be redeemed at the end of his life. If tomorrow he was gone, dead never to come back again, what would you do?"

And that was that.

Everything she said was the truth, and I needed to stop thinking so hard with my head and let my heart lead a bit.

"You're right," I admitted fully.

She smiled.

"I already knew I was right. It just took you knowing that you were."

With that I walked out my GG's door and went to find my man.

She was right.

I didn't care about what he'd done in his past.

I didn't care if he wanted to become a contract killer and hunt down men for the rest of his life.

If that time came, I'd be there when he got home.

With my arms wide open.

Now I just had to convince him that he wanted the same.

CHAPTER 14

Leg shaving season is here, and I'm not mentally prepared.

-Things that come out of Verity's mouth

Truth

I shut off my motorcycle and looked at my house.

It didn't look different, but I knew she was there.

I'd said some awful things to her the other day, so for her to be back meant that maybe I hadn't fucked things up as badly as I'd thought.

But likely, I had, and she was just here to make me feel even worse.

I swear if she was crying, I was going to apologize on my goddamned knees for years if that was what it took.

The last six days had been pure hell.

I'd said those nasty words to her, and I hadn't been able to get a hold of her since. I'd called. Texted. Sent out goddamned search parties. The men that I'd put on her couldn't find her. They reported that she never went home that night after I'd kicked her out of my bed, and I'd been a nervous wreck until she was found shopping at the goddamned mall yesterday afternoon.

Happy as could be buying goddamned lingerie of all things.

When Aaron had spotted her there while he was there with his wife, he'd immediately called me, told me where she was and said that he'd keep an eye on her until one of our prospects could get there and tail her to wherever the hell she'd been hiding.

Then he'd had fuckin' lunch with her while Aaron's wife, Imogen, and Verity had a grand ol' time talking about babies, marriages and what they wanted out of life.

To make matters worse, I'd stayed away, knowing I couldn't go and potentially expose her.

If Beckett didn't already know about Verity, which hopefully was the case, then I wanted to keep it that way.

Especially since I'd gone and fallen in love with her.

I'd just dismounted my bike when I heard someone pull up behind me.

And immediately sighed when I saw Destiny pop out of the car, followed immediately by Kenneth, who looked less than excited to be in my driveway.

I heard my front door open, and I turned to look at Verity.

She was wearing short jean shorts that likely barely covered her ass—mostly I could tell this by the fact that they were barely covering her pussy—and one of my sleeveless t-shirts that I used to work out in. It was one of those ones where the arm holes extended from the shoulder all the way to the ribs…when I was wearing it. On Verity, the hole extended from her shoulder all the way to her waist.

I could see a black lace bra underneath, tantalizing me with small glimpses of what it was covering.

Her brown hair was all the way down her back in soft waves, and part of it was clipped back with what likely was bobby pins on top of her head, ensuring that none of her bangs were in her face.

She was holding a spatula in one hand, and a bottle of beer—one of my bottles of beer—in her other hand.

She took a sip, let her eyes linger on me, before moving to Kenneth and Destiny at the end of the driveway.

"What's going on, honey?" she asked, stepping out onto the front porch.

That's when I saw her toes.

Her toenails were painted a glittery pink that was so bright that I could see them from where I was parked.

"What are you doing here?" Destiny snapped.

"I live here. What are you doing here?" Verity returned.

I chose not to call Verity on her lie. Instead, I dropped the helmet to the bike frame, then headed for the porch stairs.

The moment I came within reach, which happened to be at the bottom of the steps, Verity launched herself at me.

I caught her easily, pulling her securely into my body and closing my eyes as her scent and the feel of her body washed over me.

I didn't notice the way I rocked back on my heels when she threw herself at me.

The other two people standing there watching me did, though.

And they made it a point to comment on the fact.

"Even a big man like your ex can't handle her…"

I stiffened and turned, dropping my hold on Verity's ass as I did, and felt her go preternaturally still as she tried to figure out what I was about to do.

"Uhh," Verity started to say.

I held my hand up to stop whatever it was she was about to say.

"You come onto my land, insult my woman, and expect to make it off of this property alive?" I asked him incredulously.

Kenneth's mouth kicked up into a smirk.

"Just saying what I saw," he shrugged. "Not my fault it's true."

I took a threatening step forward, but stopped when I saw a third person get out of the car.

"Boys and girls," Eugene grumbled. "This is not the time, nor the place. You came here to say something, Destiny, so say it."

Destiny's mouth tightened.

"I'm pregnant."

Verity, who'd been leaning against my side, stiffened.

My hand clenched onto her hand and held on when she would've marched her ass back inside.

"Please," I said. "Enlighten me on how, exactly, something like that would've happened."

Destiny's mouth tightened.

"You really want me to give you the talk of the birds and bees?" she sneered. "Because I can if your big, muscled brain can't figure it out."

I laughed.

"If I use a condom, and you use your own form of birth control, how would that happen?" I repeated. "And say some sort of accident did happen, how far along are you?"

She gritted her teeth. "Five months."

I blinked.

"We broke up more than five months ago, and it'd been over two months before that that we had sex. So correct me if I'm wrong, but the timing is not good...right?"

My voice was so sarcastic that it was apparent to not just her, but even the dumbass at her side.

Destiny's eyes narrowed.

"I never said it was yours," she hissed.

I sighed and rubbed my hands down my face.

"Then what, exactly, is the problem?" I grumbled tiredly. "Why am I even involved in this?"

"Do you mind if I talk to him by myself for a few?"

Eugene's authoritative voice had me blinking in surprise. He almost sounded like a normal male—one not afraid of his own shadow.

"Sure," Kenneth grumbled, tossing Eugene an evil look.

When the two of them went to head to my front door, I stopped them.

"I don't think so," I snapped. "We'll go inside, and y'all can stay out here."

Kenneth growled low under his breath, and I had to resist the urge to laugh at the stupid fucker.

"Come on inside, man," I said, pocketing my keys since I wouldn't be needing them.

The minute I got close enough to the door, my eyes caught Verity's, and she gave me a guilty look before scampering away, leaving the door open.

I would've laughed had this situation not been seriously fucked.

Didn't she know I was trying to protect her?

Eugene followed me up the stairs of the porch, and I gestured him to precede me inside.

"What's up, Eugene?" I asked as I closed the door on the couple that was standing in the driveway looking like two complete dolts.

They were looking around, not talking to each other, and trying to act like they weren't as mad as I could so obviously tell that they were.

"I need a drink," Eugene muttered. "Once I swallow the bile back down, I'll enlighten you."

I sighed, thinking he was exaggerating a little bit, but nonetheless got him a glass of ice water and handed it to him.

He devoured it, sucking it down so fast that I immediately got him another.

"Thanks," he said, taking the second glass.

Verity, who was standing next to the sink peeling potatoes, sneaked a look at me, and immediately returned to what she was doing.

"I'm glad to see y'all are back together."

I gave him a pointed look. "Get on with it, Eugene."

He thrust his hands through his hair and took a seat at the table, dropping down so heavily that I wondered if he was sick.

Was that why he drank so much? Was he dying?

His next words had me realizing that no, he wasn't dying. Though, he may soon wish he was dead.

"I slept with Destiny a week and a half after y'all broke up, but I didn't realize that I did until I found out that I had an …STD."

I blinked.

"I'm clean," I said. "Got checked after I found out she was

cheating…why would you think this…"

He sighed.

"I'm not sure what or how it happened. I just think it's fucking comical that I catch crabs around the same time she tells me that she has crabs, and that was a day and a half after she stayed at my house," he grumbled under his breath. "I don't even know how it happened. One second I was sleeping, and the next I was having sex. I wasn't even aware that it wasn't a dream until…"

"Until you got crabs," I supplied.

Verity sounded like she choked, but I couldn't be sure without taking my eyes off of Eugene, and I suspected if I showed the least bit of reaction, he might very well flip a switch.

"And how did they even know that this baby wasn't Kenneth's?" I asked, really tired now. Was it acceptable to sleep a solid twenty-four hours? "And why are they *here*?"

"I convinced Kenneth that you might be able to help." He wiped some sweat off his brow with the back of his hand. "She came to my house, drunker than a skunk and high on…something I haven't been able to identify yet, and spent the night."

"And fucked you while you slept…"

Eugene nodded once.

"Fuckin' A. Why'd y'all have to bring me into this bullshit?"

"Because it was either bring you in, or tell Kenneth that I slept with her…and I know how much you like my face…"

Verity, who finally chose to stop hiding the fact that she was listening to every single detail, turned and surveyed Eugene's face.

"There's more to it…" Verity added in her two cents.

"The baby has a genetic anomaly that causes birth defects, and they said that if the baby makes it to term, the baby may need an immediate liver and or kidney transplant." He licked his lips.

"Why not just tell them?" she finally asked.

"Because if I tell them, then I have to tell my brother that I slept with his wife, which will inevitably cause him to beat the shit out of me. It's bad enough already. I need you to be the buffer," Eugene admitted reluctantly.

I licked my lips and turned my gaze to the tabletop.

"I still don't understand why you think I can help," I told my cousin, who was sitting there looking so forlorn that it was sad.

I was literally sad for the man and what he had to endure.

But I didn't know what else I was supposed to do. It wasn't my kid. Wasn't my wife nor my girlfriend, and Kenneth wasn't my brother. He was my cousin...a cousin who I despised.

So yeah, I couldn't really see it. And honestly, I felt no sympathy for the two outside.

The one inside, however, yeah—I didn't even know what to say to that. You didn't have to be a genius to figure out that Destiny had taken advantage of him.

How, I wasn't sure, but I would be figuring that out.

"I want you to tell him."

It came out so fast, that I had to slow down and think about what he just said.

"You want me to tell your brother that you slept with his wife, my ex-girlfriend, the woman who cheated on me with him. Do I have that correct?" I asked slowly.

Verity started to snicker from beside me, and she quickly turned to busy herself at the sink again.

She was peeling potatoes, and from what I could tell, doing a piss poor job at it since her hands and shoulders were starting to shake.

I leaned back in my chair to see what she was doing, and frowned when I saw frozen chicken thawing in the sink.

I didn't bother to ask her what she was doing, especially since I could hear my cousin's sniffles across from me.

I wanted to throw up.

"You still have crabs?" was the smart thing that came out of my mouth next.

Eugene gulped.

"No." He shook his head. "Thank God."

Verity dropped something into the sink.

I ignored her and continued to stare at my cousin.

"Are you sure that the kid's yours?"

He nodded miserably.

"Whose else could it be?"

That was when I laughed.

***

Two hours later, plenty of crying, bitching, moaning and generally bad moods around, my family left—leaving me with one last thing to deal with.

I stomped into my house, in a much worse mood than I'd been in when I'd left it two hours before, and found myself staring at a meal spread out across my dinner table and no Verity in sight.

I prowled through the house, and growled her name. "Verity!"

She didn't answer, but I knew she was here…somewhere.

Because her car was still here, and because she'd spent the last two hours silently watching the spectacle on the front porch with a look of glee on her face.

Though, it didn't matter if she had left. I would've tracked her down.

Mostly because I wanted to know why the fuck she was wearing a wedding ring on her finger—one that I sure as hell didn't give her.

She either got married in the short time since I'd last seen her, or there were some other reasons for her to be wearing it. A reason that I didn't yet understand.

"Verity!" I bellowed when I didn't find her in the bedroom or bathroom, either.

There was one last place to look, and that was my workshop.

And as I prowled down the steps and opened the door to my office, I was stunned to see it brimming with shit.

A lot of shit.

It hadn't escaped my attention that she'd moved other shit in, too.

I'd seen the new couch—and had idly wondered what she'd done with my old one.

I'd also made note of the new bed, the clothes of hers hanging in the closet, the bras hanging from the shower rod, and the new fucking ugly ass rug on the living room floor.

The big ass TV, however, was a welcome addition.

I didn't often watch TV, but when I did, I'd hated watching it on my television.

But you used what you had, and I was too cheap to go buy a new one when I could wait a couple of months and get one on sale on Black Friday.

So I'd ignored the fact that half of my TV was pixelated and shitty, and I hadn't realized how much I hated it until I'd gotten a brand new one that sat in its place.

The shop, however, was pushing things.

Her shit was shoved in there with my shit, and I could tell immediately it wasn't going to work.

She was even using my forge!

"What are you doing?" I bellowed. "Get out!"

Verity didn't bother to look over her shoulder at me. Instead, she continued to do something with the glass she had on the end of one of my goddamned pieces of metal tubing—the ones that I used to shape my swords—and stuck it back into the fire.

"You can't be here," I tried for reason. "It's not safe."

"Marriage is a matter of public record," she said bluntly to me without so much as a flinch. "All he would need to do is run a search on you, and he'll find my named linked to yours...in marriage."

"We're not married!" I barked, worry making me say it a little more harshly than I would have normally.

She smiled sympathetically at me.

"Unfortunately for you, we are," she said, getting up and emptying her pockets.

She came up with a folded piece of white computer paper, handing it to me with an apologetic look.

I opened it and froze, seeing the marriage certificate in all its glory.

"When...how...where..."

She started to laugh, then.

"Vegas, baby," was her answer. "Apparently, what happens in Vegas, doesn't always stay in Vegas."

My jaw clenched.

Her eyes studied my angry face.

"At least I'm not pregnant," she offered, thinking it'd diffuse the situation.

But the only thing it did was make my mind go wild with possibilities. If she was pregnant, I'd be ecstatic. At least until I thought about all the ugly possibilities that could happen to a child—and a wife—of mine.

"We have to get it annulled," I shook my head.

"No."

"Verity," I growled, taking a menacing step forward.

She took one of her own toward me, and then threw herself into my arms.

"I won't leave you," she said. "You could take your name back, but that would only hurt me. And you don't want to hurt me. That's what all of this is about, isn't it? You don't want me to get hurt." She leaned forward until her forehead touched mine. "You take your name from me, and that'll hurt me worse than anything you, or anyone, could ever do to me. It'll rip my heart out, and leave me bleeding and vulnerable."

CHAPTER 15

*If you love someone, just tell them. Or text them
eighteen times. It's the same thing.*

-Verity's secret thoughts

Verity

I'd been living with my husband—and yes, I still couldn't believe
that I was calling him that, let alone that he actually was—now for
a week.

I'd realized a few things.

One, he was messy.

Two, he was bossy.

Three, he was noisy.

Four, he was whiney.

Okay, maybe not that fourth one so much until just this minute.

"I'm going to work." He frowned hard at me.

I idly wondered if that frown of his worked on other people, or if it
was only me who was immune to his anger. Maybe it was because
I knew he wouldn't hurt me. Or maybe it was because I could see
the excitement in his eyes when I fought with him.

I could also see the hard column of his cock that was straining the front of his black tactical pants that he wore while he was teaching.

"I don't think you…"

"I'm. Going. To work," I repeated, much slower this time.

He sighed. "Fine."

My lips pursed.

"Why'd you give in so easily?" I demanded.

"Because I knew you were going to go in. I got yesterday out of you, but that was just by the skin of my teeth," he answered instantly. "Now, I need to tell you about the cameras and the security system. Give you emergency numbers, and a code to use if you feel you're in trouble and can't speak."

I bit my lip to keep from denying him, knowing he needed this to know I was safe.

That didn't make me feel better about being treated like a prisoner by my own husband, though.

Even if I had brought it upon myself.

I listened as he droned on and on, even taking my phone at one point to program in not just every member's number in the Dixie Wardens Alabama Chapter, but also the Benton, Louisiana chapter. A man named Silas, his son named Sebastian. A man named Kettle. Trance. Loki. Cleo. Torren and Sterling.

There were also a few men from some place in Texas, but he told me not to use them unless I'd exhausted all of the Dixie Warden resources.

"Okay," he said, handing me back my phone. "I'll go get a shower. Is there anything else you need?"

I bit my lip to keep from calling him crazy, and instead settled on shaking my head.

I even managed to keep my temper under control…all the way up until he insulted one of my favorite songs by Macklemore.

"This is the stupidest song I've ever heard," he grumbled.

"Then close your ears," I snapped.

He sighed, long and loud.

"I'm only doing this for your own good," he said to me.

"Why are we in my car, anyway?" I snapped, glaring out the window.

I knew why.

If I was insistent on going to work, he was going to be sure that I was virtually stuck there unless I called someone to come get me. And he knew I wouldn't bother him while I was at work, and he also knew that I wouldn't be leaving because I'd already been out the week prior.

So, by taking my car, he would then take it to work after dropping me off at the pub.

Effectively stranding me there until he was ready to come back and get me.

"Remember what I said about the cameras. There is one in every room, even the bathroom," he started to repeat for the fourth time that morning. "If you go in there, make sure you text me or the number I gave you so they can switch it off."

"I'm not texting you," I started to say, but he interrupted me before I could finish. "And I'll be sure to tell the prospects to pay attention. If they see you go in there, they'll know to turn it off before they see anything I don't want them to see."

I harrumphed.

"This is ridiculous," I muttered.

And it was.

But the kiss he gave me as he dropped me off in the dining room of the pub was enough to leave me weak and breathless. At least until he called halfway through the day and told me he wouldn't be back until well after closing time because something 'had come up.'

Which left me there for six hours longer than I wanted to be.

By the time he arrived an hour after closing, a long thirteen hours later, I was tired, hungry, and not in the mood to go to a club party.

Did he ask me what I wanted, though?

Hell no. He just took me straight to the clubhouse, which was so far off any main roads that I knew I would never find my way out if I happened to wrangle the keys from my man, and pulled into the longest fucking driveway in the history of mankind.

Then he wedged my car into a parking spot so small that I knew I'd have to exit out his side of the vehicle or I might hit the bike he'd parked next to, and he knew it.

Chicken shit.

I stayed there, waiting for him to get out, and finally sighed and gave him my attention.

"Thank you," he said.

"For what?" I snarled.

"For finally looking at me."

I rolled my eyes. "What did you want, your highness?"

His mouth twitched, and then his arm was around my waist and he hauled me roughly across the console before slamming his mouth down onto mine.

I gasped, unable to help the reaction my body had to his, and threaded my fingers around his neck.

He pulled back, and then opened his stupid mouth.

"Should've kissed you half an hour ago, and might've gotten you into a better mood."

I smacked him on the forehead, causing him to laugh.

He got out, and pulled me with him, and waved at another bike that pulled up behind my car.

"What's wrong with her?"

Aaron.

I turned to him and wrinkled my nose.

"I'm hungry, and tired, and my husband is an asshole," I turned back to my man. "You could've at least warned me that this was what we were doing."

"I would've, but you refused to answer my calls."

"I refused to answer your calls," I poked him in the chest. "Because you wouldn't stop calling to check on me in between every single break you took, which, might I add, was a whole lot more than normal."

He shrugged.

"I don't like you being there by yourself...especially not after...my grandfather."

I narrowed my eyes.

"Don't try to play the pity card with me," I poked him again. "Shithead."

He laughed then, making me want to smack him.

"Your hair is sticking up," he continued to dig his grave deeper.

I gave up and turned on my heel, walking straight to the back porch where I could see the now retreating back of Aaron.

I could hear Truth's footsteps behind me, and I hurried faster, but he easily kept pace with my shorter stride.

I could feel him at my back as we climbed the steps to the porch, which was suspended about twenty feet or so off the ground and were attached to the back of the large house.

I waved at those that I knew, and came to a halt at the table of food that was laid out before me.

I went for a cup of ice and the tea, resigning myself to disappointment.

"Grab yourself a plate," Truth ordered from my side.

He was already filling up his own plate, piling it so high with crab, shrimp, and corn that I worried for the integrity of the plate.

"It's seafood. It's good. I promise."

I knew it was seafood. I also knew that if I ate it, I'd be in the toilet having the fires of holy hell leaking out of my ass because it gave me diarrhea almost the moment the food hit my mouth.

So no, despite knowing they were good, I wouldn't be eating them.

"No thanks," I shook my head in the negative.

It was just my luck that the entire get together was based around a crab boil—something that also made my colon want to eject from my body.

I also couldn't eat the potatoes or corn since they'd been boiled with the crab and shrimp.

"Come on, try it, you'll like it." He waved the shrimp in front of my nose.

I bared my teeth.

"If I eat it," I said lowly so only he could hear. "I'll spend the entire night on the potty trying not to shit my guts out…okay?"

He clamped his mouth shut, finally realizing that everything here was along the same lines as the shrimp.

"I'll go get you something…"

I left him before he could finish, heading straight to the table where the ladies were sitting and dropping in next to Aaron's wife, Imogen.

"Men are stupid," I told her.

She snorted before taking a drink from her red Solo cup.

"I think you should meet my husband," Tally said. "He's an ass on a good day. On a bad day, well let's just say he's…"

"Let's just say what?"

That was Tommy, her husband, and I had to bite my lip to keep from laughing at the look on Tally's face.

"He's an even bigger ass," Tally finished. "Why are you skulking?"

Tommy's mouth kicked up, and I saw his hand lower behind Tally's back, and she shivered.

"What do you think he just did?" Imogen whispered.

"My guess is that he just put his hands down her pants," I whispered right back.

Tally's eyes, which had been unfocused and distant, finally returned to me.

"But there's this thing about the man you love," she whispered, not caring that the man she loved was standing at her back, listening to every word. "They can drive you insane, but at the end of the night, when you're in their arms, everything that was wrong with that day ceases to exist."

I found my first smile since I'd arrived.

The happiness that I could see on her face was reflected on his, and I felt a pang of sadness hit me.

Would I ever have that with Truth? Or had I forced myself on him, and we'd never have that?

I didn't know, but I hoped like hell that one day we would—if only we could get over the Elais Beckett hurdle, I felt like we would have a fighting chance.

Hiding my irritation as well as I could, I settled on nibbling on the cookies that were lining the table as far as the eye could see.

"You're freakin' awesome, you know that?"

I took another bite of cookie and smiled at Imogen.

"Why do you say that?" I asked.

"Because you've just eaten your seventh cookie, and haven't slowed down long enough to care about the fact that the men are watching you like you you're going to go postal any moment."

I sighed.

Looking down at the cookies with disgust, I shoved the next two into my mouth and made a promise to myself that I'd lose the weight I'd put on since moving into the same house as Truth.

It wasn't a lot of weight, per se, but it was enough that I couldn't fit into my jeans as well as I'd been able to do two weeks ago.

I looked over at the man responsible for all my weight gain—all seven pounds of it—and let my eyes rove all over his body.

Even in a pair of jeans, a black shirt, and his cut, the man looked ripped. He looked like he worked out, played hard and had no regrets at all in life.

His eyes turned away from the conversation he was having with

Seanshine, Aaron, and Tommy—*when had he left?*—and caught mine. Our gazes caught and held.

"Have y'all gotten serious?"

I looked up, and realized rather quickly that the ladies were having a conversation around me—one that clearly was about me—and I hadn't been paying the least bit of attention.

"I'm sorry, what?" I gave Tally a small, apologetic smile.

"I asked if y'all were serious."

I looked down at my ring, fingering it, and the ladies gasped.

"What is that?" Tally grabbed my hand.

Imogen leaned across the table, her ass waving in the air, and snatched my hand to hers.

"You're married?" Imogen shrieked.

***

Truth

I was having a serious conversation with Aaron about emergency protocols, my hand on Tank's head, petting him softly, when the woman's shrieks rent the air.

"You're married?" Imogen shrieked.

The men that were surrounding me looked in my direction, wondering if I would deny it, but I could do nothing but shrug.

"Vegas, baby."

The men had, apparently, neglected to tell their wives that we were married.

Big Papa snorted.

"Got my first wife that way, too."

175

We'd all heard about Big Papa's first wife.

She was a Vegas show dancer and had seen him at a show. She thought he was some big man made of money with him dressed up so fancy as he was. Really he'd just been attending a police officer's convention and had worn a suit instead of his uniform. Tracy, Big Papa's first wife, thought he was hot shit in that suit, and one thing led to another, causing them to be married by the end of the night.

Sean came along nine months later, and two months after that, she was gone again, never to be seen again.

Big Papa had filed for divorce, and had then filed for abandonment when nothing ever came of the divorce papers he'd sent to her.

Six months later, Big Papa was officially a single father, and he'd pretty much been that way ever since.

Though he'd been married one other time, but that hadn't taken either.

That one had just been a fast and loose wedding as well. The marriage had been even shorter.

Two days after Lizzibeth married Big Papa, she filed for an annulment.

But that was about all I knew about that one.

Lizzibeth had nearly broken Big Papa.

It didn't seem like too big a deal at the time, but now that I had a woman of my own, I could see the lines on his face. I could also read the loneliness in his eyes, though he'd never admit to it.

"Well, I'll be damned," Aaron said, popping me solidly on the back with one scarred hand. "The real question is, what are you going to do about it."

I sighed.

"I'm not doing anything about it," I admitted. "I'm going to keep living my life."

"And what about her?"

That was from Ghost.

"What's it to you if I do anything or not?" I shot back.

"What's it to me?" he asked, leaning forward out of the shadows. "You have a woman that cares for you, and you're just going to throw her away?"

I'd never said that. Not even once.

"Nope," I denied. "She's already moved into my house. Now I just have to make sure that pecker head doesn't try to kill her."

"That won't happen," Big Papa promised, ready to turn the topic at hand. "Now, about that security."

I listened, and even retained some of the information, but it was hard to keep my hands off my woman…my wife.

She was talking animatedly to Imogen and Tally about something, and the way her eyes swung from one woman to the other, paired with the smile on her face, was making me lose concentration.

"Earth to Lover Boy," Sean drawled.

I sighed and returned my attention back to the conversation at hand.

And immediately wished I hadn't.

"We're going to make a run this weekend to the Benton Chapter House," Big Papa was saying. "You are not cordially invited. You're going, along with the rest of us."

"Can the women go?" I asked.

Aaron groaned.

Tommy grinned.

"We already went over that, for about fifteen minutes," Sean said. "This is a penis only trip, and vaginas aren't invited."

"But what about Beckett?" I asked. "I can't leave her here by herself with that jerkwad loose in this town."

Big Papa continued to stare.

"We went over that, too." Sean confirmed.

I crossed my arms over my chest.

"And what was decided?"

"That we send the women for a girls' weekend up north," Tommy said. "My parents are living in Colorado for the winter. They want to partake in unlimited snowboarding and have a place big enough to house not only the ladies, but us as well if we want to drive there after we're done here."

I thought about it.

"I do have a break coming between sessions," I admitted. "I have to finish a sword, and the next one up after that is Verity's project for her dad. If I ask her to go to Colorado, and tell her I'll join her there in a few days, she won't have a problem with that."

Big Papa slapped me on the back.

"It's settled then." He stood up. "Who wants to take a shot with me?"

Nobody raised their hand, and Big Papa laughed.

"Never thought I'd see the day where all of my boys are pussy whipped."

With that parting comment, he left, leaving Sean, me, Tommy, and Aaron sitting around an unlit fire pit, staring at each other.

"I'm not pussy whipped," Sean finally added. "I don't even have pussy."

We all let that digest for a few long moments before Tommy chimed in with, "That sounds pretty sad."

"I thought you were into Tommy's sister?"

That came from one of the prospects, and everyone around the fire pit tensed.

I looked at Tommy to gauge his reaction. Aaron looked at Sean.

And I chose to leave.

Ghost chose to follow me.

I had a destination in mind.

Ghost followed me because it was either stay and listen to drama between brothers, or listen to women...and I knew which one I would rather have.

I lifted my hand and grasped onto Verity's pony tail, tipping her head backwards with a slight tug.

"You ready to go?" I asked.

She blinked, and then let her eyes drift over to Ghost.

"Yes," she answered. "But I told the ladies that they could come over tomorrow so we could make cookies for the firefighters stew and auction tomorrow night."

I looked over at Ghost, who shrugged.

We both knew that the ladies weren't going to miss this stew and auction without a great bit of coercion on our part.

"About that..."

CHAPTER 16

*When you're feeling powerless, just remember
one thing. A single one of your pubic hairs will
shut down an entire restaurant.*

-Fact of Life

Verity

I woke up early to cook the Motley Crew, also known as Sean
(Seanshine I'd heard him called last night), Ghost (a scary man
who was eerily quiet and rather intimidating), and my husband
breakfast.

I was still fuming.

So, not only did he not feed me anything but cookies all night long,
but he'd also given explicit orders that we were leaving for
Colorado tomorrow afternoon, and we would miss the firefighters
stew and auction.

Something that I'd gone to every year for the last five years.
Something that I adored going to because it made me feel happy to
see the excitement on the firefighters' faces when they saw my
donation check.

I'd just finished up with the last of the bacon and was cutting it
into pieces to mix in with the scrambled eggs, when Truth came in.

He looked rough.

And not just the normal rough that he always looked, but an even rougher rough that made him look more caveman than man.

"Wow," I said, eyeing his beard. "Did you at least brush your teeth?"

He bared said teeth at me, and I grinned.

Then frowned.

"Why do you smell like onions?" I asked him.

He took a seat at the kitchen table where all the food was laid out and frowned.

"After you went to bed last night, Sean went to grab us some burgers from The Warehouse. I ate two," he said, poking the eggs with his finger. "I'm not hungry at all."

The knife I was using to cut the bacon with hit the counter with a clash, causing him to look up.

"You *what*?" I said carefully, turning fully to look at him.

"I said, Sean grabbed us some burgers from The Warehouse," he repeated, not understanding that he was in danger. "Ghost and Sean aren't hungry either."

"Why would you do that?" I asked. "And if you were to go out and get food, why would you not have at least offered to bring me some?"

"Because you were asleep?" he said slowly. *Carefully.*

I most certainly had not been asleep. In fact, I'd been watching TV when he'd come into our bedroom, and I had been meaning to ask him for hours why he smelled like onions, but I hadn't wanted to wake him up.

Now, I realized, I shouldn't have been so considerate. It was obvious that he wasn't.

I gently picked up what was left of the bacon, and walked it over to the trashcan, before dumping it inside.

I'd already had a protein shake, and I'd only gone through the torture of making the most delicious smelling bacon in the world for his ass.

And now he said he didn't want it.

Fucking wonderful.

"What the hell?" Truth asked, watching me reach for the eggs.

I took them and dumped them into the trash, too.

Eighteen eggs and twenty-five pieces of bacon, ruined.

My mother would've had a conniption.

And without another word, I walked out of the kitchen and to the bedroom, closing it quietly behind me before sitting on the bed and trying not to cry.

What the fuck was wrong with me? Me, Verity Ruthann Cassidy, no Verity Ruthann Reacher, crying over a goddamned hamburger, bacon and eggs?

I seriously needed to get a grip, but I couldn't.

I continued to stay mad at him, even when he said the sweetest words I'd ever heard him say two hours later as he was preparing to leave me.

"If I only had one helmet, I would give it to you," he told me.

I managed to hold a straight face, but just barely.

He left me with a peck on the cheek, and then he was gone.

I sat there, wondering whether I'd made a mistake.

But no answers were forthcoming.

Sighing and standing up to start packing, I busied myself with folding clothes and rearranging Truth's sword collection in his closet so I didn't have to think about matters of the heart.

***

"He even quoted my favorite song!" I yelled, clapping my hands twice to get the ladies attention back.

"That's ground for divorce," Tally said. "You should serve him papers."

I snorted.

"I'm just kidding," Tally sighed and picked up her own suitcase, hefting it into the back of Imogen's SUV before shutting the hatch.

"Do you think they'll leave us once we get to the city line?" Imogen asked, eyeing the four prospects who were idling on their bikes behind us.

"Probably not," I muttered. "Because if they leave us, then I'm unprotected."

"Don't feel special. Aaron still has them follow me around periodically, too. If I don't answer my phone fast enough, the first thing he does is send one of them in my direction, if he doesn't come himself." She smiled. "They're overprotective. You're just going to have to learn to live with it."

I shrugged.

"I will. It's just tough, because I'm not used to having someone shadow my every move. They're with me at the grocery store. They followed me into the feminine hygiene product aisle two days ago. They even tried to come into the bathroom with me. When I opened it and showed them it was a single stall without a window, they reluctantly backed off. Though I'm sure if I'd have let them come in they would have."

Imogen snickered.

Tally, however, turned in the front seat and looked at me.

"Tommy told me a little bit about this Elais Beckett guy."

I swallowed, and then nodded. "Yeah?"

She twisted her fingers as she explained.

"Tommy said that Truth was in a bad place when he got home from his last mission. Shut himself in his house or his workshop, and stayed there for close to a month. It wasn't until Stone…"

I held up my hand to stop her. "Who is Stone?"

Her face fell a little bit more. "Stone was the Dixie Warden's old president. The cop who was killed by the gang member nearly a year ago."

My heart fell.

"I never knew he was involved with the MC," I whispered. "I was gone the week it happened for a wedding in New Hampshire. I heard about it on Fox News, though. I couldn't believe something like that happened in our small town."

Tally licked her lips then continued. "Stone forced him to think straight again. Apparently, when he found him, Truth was a mess. He'd built eight swords in a one-week span, and you know how long those take him to get done."

Months. He had to stay up night and day to get even one done. For him to get that many done in such a short time span was likely not conducive with Truth's health.

I started to feel worse.

"Vengeance was his answer, though, to pulling his head out of his ass. He was in a dark place, and Tommy said he was kind of scary while he was doing whatever he did during the time he was working with Elais Beckett."

Doing whatever he was doing meant killing people.

I shuddered.

I didn't judge the man. I knew he was just doing his job, something he believed in and thought was right. He didn't know that Elais Beckett was giving him inaccurate information to manipulate him into doing his bidding.

"Hey, how about we go to eat?"

My head swung up, and I realized we'd left my driveway, and had gone as far as the city limits. The city limits where the fire station sat, with hundreds of cars parked around the station.

"Yes," I said instantly. "I vote yes."

Tally and Imogen laughed, and then Imogen swung her car into the only available spot, which, luckily enough, happened to be very close to the building.

The four bikers that were following us pulled directly in behind us and idled, wondering what we were going to do.

When we got out and started heading for the front door, and the mass of people, they jumped off their bikes and headed toward us.

"I bet we're giving them minor heart attacks right now," Imogen murmured quietly just before the four of them showed up at our sides.

I, of course, had two. One on each side of me.

The one on my right was on the smaller side, and he had a quick smile, especially when he saw me looking.

"What's your name?" I asked.

"Fender."

I blinked.

"Your real name is Fender, or your 'road name' is Fender?"

He had a really great smile.

"My road name is Fender. I was two days into pledging as a prospect when I fell and hit my head on the fender of a car. I got this exciting little scar to commemorate it. The members haven't let me live it down yet," he chuckled to himself.

"Watch out," a man took my arm. The other prospect on my side.

I looked down at the large hand guiding me around a huge rut in the dirt that would've made me bust my ass had he not moved me, and then back up at the other prospect.

This one I didn't know anything about, and I didn't get the happy vibes off of him that I got off of Fender.

No, this man was scary.

Not in a 'he's going to kill me' way, but in a 'he could kill me if he wanted to' kind of way.

His name was Jessie James, and yes, that was his real name. I'd asked Truth that in the few words I'd allowed him this morning before he'd left.

His answer had been short and sweet. "His name is Jessie James, we call him JJ for short. Please don't tease him about his name. It brings up bad shit for him."

"Thank you, Jessie," I said.

"JJ," he said deeply.

Man, he had a very deep voice.

"Y'all do realize that we're going to get our asses kicked for this, right?" Fender asked as he opened the door to the station and ushered us inside.

"They expected us to stop," I told him. "Or at least they should have."

Fender gave me a wink.

"We knew you'd stop," he said. "That's why there are four of us."

I refused to think that my man knew me that well…or that he was that considerate.

But by the end of the night, when we were boarding our plane to Colorado, I realized that he was very considerate.

Considerate enough to book me into first class, and considerate enough to know exactly when I was set to arrive in Colorado, and to have a freakin' car there waiting.

Yes, I decided. I did have a good one.

I still had to teach him a few lessons about having a woman in his life, though.

CHAPTER 17

*Life would be a lot more fun if everyone's middle
name was motherfuckin'.*

-Fact of Life

Truth

"That was the weirdest fucking visit I've had in my life," I grunted. "Was there a reason for what happened there?"

Ghost kept looking over his shoulder like he was a goddamned addict who'd stolen from a drug dealer. He was jumpy, his speech was rushed, and I was fairly sure that he was about to have an aneurysm if he continued to hold his breath like that.

"What's the deal, man?" I asked, stopping. "Are you okay?"

He ignored me and kept walking, coming to a stop at the shadow of the airport entrance.

"I thought I saw someone."

"Who?" I asked.

He seemed to contemplate what he was going to say for a few short moments, then he answered shortly.

"Nobody."

I looked behind me.

"You're so fuckin' confusing."

Ghost's mouth twitched, but he remained silent.

I was set to continue to question him when a roar of motorcycles drowned out the still night air around us.

Silas, the president of the Dixie Warden's Benton, Louisiana chapter, shut off his bike and dismounted.

His son, Sebastian, got off his as well and walked up to us.

"Ghost, you got a minute?"

Sebastian, who hadn't seen Ghost behind me, froze, his eyes going so wide that it was nearly comical, before he opened his mouth to say something.

"Not a fuckin' word," Silas growled. "We'll talk later."

Sebastian's mouth snapped shut, but his eyes remained on Ghost as he walked around the corner of the airport with Silas and disappeared.

"You know," I said to the big man. "I'd fuckin' love to know what the hell is going on."

Sebastian's lips twitched. "I would, too."

I had a feeling that he knew a whole lot more than I did, but who was I to argue? If I was meant to know, I'd know.

"What're y'all doing here?" I asked.

We'd spent a full day with Silas, his son, and his other club members. We'd gotten zero accomplished.

Another chapter was set to open up in Texas, and a few of the closest club members were meeting to see who wanted to help lead the new chapter.

When no volunteers were forthcoming, a vote was taken.

I wasn't chosen.

Because I was now married.

Thank God for small things. Those who were married and already had lives established in their territories weren't under consideration in those votes.

Not to mention that I wasn't moving to fucking Texas.

I was an Alabama boy, born and bred, and I wasn't big on moving to Texas, at all. Especially now that I had a wife to come home to.

"At the time, I wasn't aware of why we were coming. Now that I'm here, I see why."

His eyes stayed on where Silas and Ghost had disappeared, and I knew exactly what he was getting at.

I was like Curious fucking George. I wanted to walk over there and see what the hell was going on, but I knew if I did, Silas or Ghost would kick my ass.

I wasn't a small man, not by any means, but those two motherfuckers were mean. Both of them had this dangerous aura that always seemed to surround them, and my life had been a lesson in knowing when not to fuck with something dangerous.

Danger recognized danger after all.

"Hey, could you make me a sword for my dad for Christmas?"

I blinked, turning to find him standing almost directly next to me.

"Sure," I said. "Why?"

He snorted.

"Because my father has anything and everything he could ever imagine, and I saw that sword you gave to Torren last year. It was fucking sweet."

Pride in my work swelled in me, and I nodded once before heading to my bike.

"Y'all's boys are going to take these home, right?"

Sebastian started to chuckle. "Yes. We have prospects for…"

"No fucking prospect is going to touch my bike. You promise me that, motherfucker. I've already had one bitch fucking another cocksucker on my bike, and now I have to ride this one. If you take my spare out, then I'm boned."

Sebastian's amused eyes turned to the bike.

"I heard about that. But I also heard that you lucked out in the end."

I did.

Fuckin' A, I sure as hell did.

"How's your wife and kids doing?"

"Busy," he answered. "You'll find out soon when you start having kids. Time seems to sped up. I swear it was just last month that my daughter was born, but now she's a fucking hellion and I'm trying to keep up with her while she kicks a goddamn ball around the yard."

The thought of having kids didn't scare the shit out of me like it once did. Now all it did was make me feel fucking happy inside, like a goddamn man that was finally happy with the life he now was living.

And I guess, after contemplation, that was true. I was happy. I was happy to have Verity in my house, warming my bed. I liked the idea of her pregnant with our kids. I was actually looking forward to seeing her belly swell with my child growing inside of her.

What I was really happy about, though?

That was simple.

The fact that she chose to stay with me. That she was putting the effort in, despite my attempts at trying to put distance between us. That, in all honesty, she was putting her life in my hands.

She knew I'd keep her safe, and I would.

I'd fight until my dying breath to keep her safe.

That didn't mean that I wanted to do that…that I wanted to put her into a position where I would have to do that, but if it came down to it, and I had to give my life for hers, I'd do it. Because my life for hers seemed like one hell of a trade.

Lani Lynn Vale

CHAPTER 18

*I couldn't help but notice that I would like to
have sex with you on a regular basis.*

-A note from Verity to Truth

Verity

I woke up to lips on my neck.

Hands on my body.

A cock working its way inside of me.

But it was okay. I didn't panic, even when that huge cock shifted, going from partially inside of me to all the way inside of me in a matter of seconds.

I gasped and turned my face, burying it deeply in the bend of Truth's neck.

"Truth!" I gasped against his skin, my legs tightening around his hips.

How he had gotten this far into the process without me waking was questionable, but when he started to move his hips, tiny slight movements that let me know just how far and deep he was inside of me, I lost my ability to think coherently.

"You're awake," came his deep rumbly voice against my ear. "Took you long enough."

I bit his neck, and his hips jerked, making me smile.

He growled roughly, then clenched onto my hips with both hands as he started to fuck me harder and faster than I'd ever been fucked before.

Gone were the slow, sensuous movements and in their place was the familiar rough, erratic need that always seemed to come from the both of us.

I was seconds away from coming when Truth started to speak. He didn't stop…just interrupted.

"Baby."

I shook my head, my eyes rolling into the back of my skull.

"Baby."

Someone was knocking on the door. That's what must be causing him to stop. To slow his pace.

That orgasm that I could feel on the verge of breaking through slowly started to dissipate.

Why was he trying to talk in a moment like this? Why not just finish? Fuck whoever was at the door.

"Verity."

He growled, low and deep, and I opened my eyes. To…nothing?

The knocking still remained, though, leaving me to question what exactly was going on. Clearly, I'd been having some happy time as evidenced by my hand down my pants. I'd also been tossing and turning because my linens and comforter were down by my feet. Half on, half off, the bed.

The knocking sounded again, and I plucked my hand from my panties, jackknifed out of bed, and nearly tripped on my shoes that I'd left on the floor.

Once catching myself, I grabbed my sleep pants that I'd discarded near the wall, and slipped them on before reaching for the lock on the door.

The moment I got it open, I found the door pushed open, and my back against the wall with two hundred and forty pounds of man flesh in my hands.

"Fuck, but I missed you."

And this time, everything that happened was more than real.

By the time he showed me just how real, I was on the floor with my head halfway under the bed. The pretty chevron bed skirt was covering half my face, and I found myself wondering if this was how life was going to go for me from now on.

Were we always going to have sex this good? Was Truth just some sex master who just knew how to manipulate women's bodies or were we special?

My hope was that we were special together.

"I'm sorry."

His sincere apology had me blinking in surprise.

"What?" I asked, startled.

He pulled out of me, slapped a towel on my vagina, and yanked me out from under the bed by my hips.

I gasped, the carpet burning my back and ass, and glared.

"Ouch," I snapped. "Gently, motherfucker."

He snorted.

"I said, I'm sorry," he repeated again.

"Why?" I asked suspiciously.

"What do you mean, why?"

His brows lowered, and he looked at me for a few long seconds before sighing and offering me his hand.

I took it, and he hauled us both up by our feet at the same time.

The man was amazingly in shape, and I felt like a lard ass next to him.

But he didn't seem to care about my lard, nor my carpet burned ass.

His eyes were worried, and I waited for him to say whatever it was he was trying not to say.

"I'm not very good at this husband thing," he admitted finally.

I waited for more, but none was forthcoming.

Leaning to the side so I could waddle and hold the towel at the same time, I walked to the bathroom and cleaned myself up before responding.

"I'm not very good at being a wife."

He snorted and followed close behind me.

"We're going to bungle through this together then," he said as he gathered my naked body into his.

"What was the meeting in Louisiana about?" I asked, curious as hell to see what he would say.

Would he tell me the truth? I already had the truth…at least what I knew to be the truth. Jessie—no *JJ*—had told me that it was some meeting about moving to Texas and starting a new chapter.

I wondered if he had been assigned to there. JJ had also told me that the decision wouldn't be their call. If they were asked to go, they'd have to go.

And I kind of wanted to.

There was nothing holding me here. I didn't have a job—not really. Sure, Truth was currently keeping me employed, but it wasn't like it was something that I really needed to be there for. I was there as moral support. The pub ran like a well-oiled machine, and I was sure if I left, they wouldn't notice I was missing.

They hadn't in that week I'd been gone and avoiding Truth.

In fact, I'd gotten there to check over our incoming merchandise lists, and it'd already been done. Nobody would tell me directly, but I assumed it was Truth who'd done it because nobody else had the files and passwords to get in but him—the same person to give me them in the first place.

"It's been decided to open up a new chapter in Texas, and we were asked for volunteers to see who would like to go up there and start it. The volunteers wouldn't have to stay, but it would be something that would last about six to eight months while the club established its roots and made sure everything was smoothed out in the city before we pulled out and left the remaining members to carry on without us," Truth offered without hesitation.

"And did you volunteer?" I asked hesitantly.

He shook his head and reached for his jeans.

"Fuck no," he said as he slid them on.

He didn't bother with a shirt. And he barely bothered with his pants seeing as he didn't worry to do up the belt.

The pants hung low on his hips. So low, in fact, that his happy trail and those little indents on either side of his groin were showing, making me wonder if it was possible to go again after the orgasm that I'd just had.

And as I watched him bend and twist, moving about the room as he unloaded his pocket and got rid of his belt, I realized that yes, it was indeed possible to go again in such a short amount of time.

I knew he knew how I was feeling, too. The way he watched me watch him had me nearly reaching for his pants—if I hadn't been interrupted by another freakin' knock on the door.

"This is ridiculous," I groaned. "How fucking hard is it to let a woman sleep in?"

I hadn't been able to sleep in in over a decade.

The job at the newspaper had practically forced me into being an early riser whether I wanted to be or not.

"That would be our breakfast," he grinned.

I grabbed the first thing I saw, which happened to be Truth's t-shirt, and slipped it on over my head before sitting down on the bed and pulling up my discarded covers.

My anger at being interrupted disappeared just as fast as it rose, leaving me wondering what that secret smile was on his face.

What was he smiling about?

The answer came really quickly as he opened the door, smiled at some woman who I hadn't met the night before and took the tray of food the woman was holding out to him.

She was an older woman with graying brown hair, bright blue eyes, and a sharp intellect that told me she knew exactly what she'd interrupted, and what we'd been doing in here all morning.

"Thank you, Millie," Truth said to the woman.

The woman smiled at that husband of mine like she knew him, flicked a glance my way, and then left without a word.

"Who was that?" I asked as I threw the covers off and walked toward the door where Truth had placed the tray of food on the entryway table.

"That," he said, lifting the lid off the plates and tossing them carelessly to the ground in the way only a man could, and waved his hands at the feast before him like he'd made the shit himself.

"Voila!" he said. "Does this make me a better husband yet?"

The way he was smiling at me like he'd just uncovered the Holy Grail had a grin playing at my lips.

"Yeah," I agreed readily, "it does."

He winked at me, causing my smile to widen, and brought the huge stack of pancakes to the bed and placed them on the mattress before going back for the syrup.

I bit my lip when he poured it on so thickly that it nearly ran off the plate.

"Holy shit," I said. "I hope that's yours and not mine."

I eyed the plate, waited for it to roll off the edge, but it never did.

It was like he put this much syrup on every time he had pancakes, and knew just the exact amount needed to satisfy him.

"It's mine," he said. "Though, I guess if I were a better husband, I would've allowed you to use the syrup first."

I rolled my eyes and decided that since he was in such a good mood, I wanted to ask him something that the ladies and I had discussed last night while we'd driven to Tommy's parents' place.

"I want to take engagement pictures," I broached the subject carefully. Because I knew if I worded this wrong, he would totally say no. Truth was like that with his looks. They were beautiful, and wonderful, and they were all part of the reason he hated his dad— because he looked just like him. Part of the reason he'd had such a shitty childhood.

Something I'd learned over the last few days I'd been living with him.

He didn't own a freakin' mirror, and when I'd broached the subject, he'd flat out refused to have one in the house.

When I'd gotten one anyway, he'd hidden it from me.

When I'd gotten a second one, he'd hidden that, too.

A few nights ago, we'd had a knock-down, drag out fight, and he'd finally explained that he didn't need a mirror to know what he looked like. When I'd asked why, he'd then went on to explain how, in high school, he'd been teased about being 'pretty' and over time, he'd learned to just deal.

And by dealing, that meant not doing a damn thing when it came to his appearance. That equaled no mirrors anywhere in the house, and a beard that was unruly if he didn't go to the barber shop and get it trimmed and corralled back into the beauty that it was at this very second.

Truth's eyes came to me.

"Why?" he asked suspiciously.

I smiled. "Because, in fifty years, I want to look back at these photos and remember what made them so special."

"We're already married," he pointed out.

I shrugged. "Please?"

I made sure to stick my lip out for added emphasis, and he growled low in his throat.

"Fine."

I clapped my hands excitedly.

"Oh, goody!" I said. "I know just the person!"

I'd discussed it with Tommy's mother last night, and she'd told me that there was a photographer who would likely be willing to do it if she asked.

I reached my hands around his neck and pulled him to me, placing my lips gently against his.

He tasted like syrup.

"Thank you, big guy," I placed one more kiss on his lips. "You're the greatest."

* * *

"So, this wasn't what I was thinking," I mumbled darkly.

Truth's eyes showed mirth, and it took everything I had to hold onto the pissed off look on my face.

"Oh, yeah?" he asked. "What did you have in mind?"

He grabbed my hair and pulled me forward, and I had to fight not to go limp at the feeling of his strong hand in my hair.

"I thought you'd have on nice clothes. I also thought that you'd stand here and look nice. Not hide your face every single time she went to take a picture of us."

His smile was slow, easy, and uncaring.

"Yeah?" He licked his lips, which in turn caused him to lick mine due to our close proximity. "Well, you wanted them. You said nothing about me having to look at the camera. She'll get plenty of good ones, I promise."

He was right. Each time she asked us to move to a new pose, and we did, she'd show us the pictures afterwards.

None of them had Truth's full face in the frame. None of them had his eyes.

However, in all of them, I could see the love shining in my eyes. I could also see the way Truth's body leaned over mine. How he held me protectively in his arms. How each and every shot she got, the desire he felt for me was written all over his body.

So no, I didn't have his face.

But I did have his heart, his body, and his love in the pictures, and that was enough.

As long as I had him, it would always be enough.

CHAPTER 19

One does not simply survive a June Bug attack.

-Fact of life

Verity

The boys could drink their beer, and they could handle it.

I'd witnessed all of them, even Truth, drinking at least four bottles of beer. And I say at least because I don't know for sure. I was on my third margarita, so I couldn't really tell how many they'd had since I was unable to think clearly past my own alcohol-induced haze.

However, when I was able to count, which, might I add, wasn't right now, I'd brought them all four a piece.

Why I'd been the one getting up and getting them beers was beyond me, but that was over a half an hour ago. And upon delivering the last round from the beer fridge that Tommy's parents had on the back patio, Truth told me not to deliver them any more.

Though my deliveries had stopped, they had not.

"So, what was your wedding like?" Tally asked.

I pulled out my phone and pulled up our wedding photos, ones that'd been in the packet that I'd managed to avoid looking at for months.

"I don't remember, but I have pictures," I said, turning my phone around for them to see.

"What were you wearing?" Imogen leaned forward so she could get a closer look.

"That was my wedding dress. The one that I specifically picked out to wear to my cheating ex-fiancé's wedding."

Imogen blinked.

"You know," she said. "I heard about Truth's girlfriend cheating, but I hadn't realized that your fiancé had cheated on you, too."

I nodded.

The same memories that used to make me sick now made me smile.

Not because I was happy that Kenneth had cheated, but because I was happy that he'd made it possible for me to find Truth.

Though, as humiliating as it was, I had to admit had he not done what he did, I'd be in a very different place right now. Possibly married and miserable.

Now I was married and happy, and that's the way I liked it.

"Well, have I got a story for you," I started in, not stopping until they had all the nitty gritty details.

"That's the best thing I've ever heard," Tally finally admitted. "Did he really say those things in front of all of the wedding guests?"

I nodded. "And you haven't even heard the best part. Destiny's pregnant…with her brother-in-law's baby."

They blinked, then Tally reached forward and downed the rest of her drink.

"That's just amazing," Tally finally said once she'd recovered from drinking half a Fuzzy Nipple in one gulp. "That's shit you see on Maury or Jerry Springer."

I nodded my head. "Yep."

I was reaching for my drink—which was very close to being empty—when a weird sound had me turning to track where it was coming from.

It was my purse.

Frowning, I leaned forward and stuck my hand into it, searching for the elusive buzzing that I'd never heard coming from my purse before.

"Isn't that one of those phones that was exploding?" Imogen asked as she relaxed back into her seat.

I shrugged.

I had no clue. I knew that there was a phone that was exploding, but I had no clue what it looked like.

And, apparently, it looked like the phone I'd seen Truth deposit into my purse just before coming outside.

I reached for it, slid my finger to the side, and answered the phone. "Hello?"

"Who is this?"

Destiny.

Jesus Christ.

"You know exactly who this is, you dumb bitch."

Tally and Imogen started to laugh, and I shot them 'be quiet' looks as I shushed them.

"Listen," Destiny sniffled. "Just let me talk to Truth. I need him."

My gut clenched.

I could hear that she was actually upset, but Truth wasn't hers anymore. She didn't get to call him when she was having a problem.

"How about you call your husband?" I snapped viciously.

"I can't," Destiny cried. "Because he's dead."

CHAPTER 20

*You can train a cat to do anything the cat wants
to do when the cat wants to do it.*

-Fact of Life

Truth

I was at another funeral.

In less than six weeks.

One more family member had died; this was now getting out of hand.

Kenneth hadn't been anyone special to me, and my old boss, Beckett had known it. He'd done it because he knew I'd know who it was, and he knew I'd be angry—not because Kenneth was someone I cared about, but because Kenneth was mine. He was my blood. And Beckett knew I'd know who did it.

Though it was kind of hard to miss seeing, as Kenneth was executed the exact same way my grandmother and grandfather had been.

Though, this time, Beckett had done him in the middle of a busy intersection. While Kenneth had been in his underwear.

Forty-five people had seen the execution from their cars, and dispatchers had been on the phone with two motorists when the gunshot had sounded.

Though, no one could identify Beckett. He'd been in head to toe black, it'd been dark as fuck outside with only the traffic lights to offer what little illumination there was, and he'd fled the scene on foot, disappearing into a copse of trees.

Why he'd done what he'd done to Kenneth was still a mystery, and one I was determined to figure out. He could've taken out any number of people and I'd have been more affected, but he hadn't…and I wanted to know why.

But the answers would have to wait.

Especially since I now had my father to deal with…*again*.

It didn't bode well for me that he'd come.

My father didn't even have any affiliation with Kenneth. Kenneth was kin to my mother—who hadn't come. Though I could tell there was something going on there, too.

I hadn't been able to get a hold of my mother since the funeral, and that meant only one thing. She was ignoring my calls—which she wouldn't do because, no matter how much my father liked to call me a killer, I was her baby and always would be. The other option would be that she didn't know that Kenneth had been killed, and she would likely have a conniption when she did find out.

My bet was on door number two.

My father had somehow kept this from my mother.

My father didn't know how to deal with his wife. It'd been this way since I was a young child.

My mother was not a pushover—at least not to anyone but my father. She wasn't someone that couldn't handle what she needed to handle. Yet, my father treated her as if she were a delicate flower that would blow over at the first sign of an impending storm.

My dad had been in the Marines when he'd met my mother, who'd been in the Army.

They'd both been on leave, and had stumbled upon each other at a party that was being thrown by a mutual friend. My mother and father had hit it off, and eventually my mother's love for my father won out over her desire to be active army, and she retired.

That was about how the rest of her life went. Her bowing down to my father. My father demanding it, and my mother doing it for the good of her marriage or her kids' happiness.

Which equaled my mother being a doormat for the last thirty-something years that she'd been married to my father, and us kids having to witness the disaster.

Like right now, for instance.

My father was sitting on the outside of the pew, followed by Marnie, Abel, Verity and then me.

Marnie had been told that she had a day and a half max and that she would not be getting any more leave time, no matter who passed away.

Everyone was silent as the preacher said the final prayer and then gestured for the funeral home pallbearers to carry the coffin to the door.

Destiny, wiping tears from her face, followed the pallbearers, and didn't look at anyone on her way out the door.

Kenneth's mother, Eugene, and his father walked close behind, expressionless faces telling me nothing.

I got up and offered Verity my hand, and she took it, leaning into me.

I squeezed her hip, admiring the way she filled out her dress, and urged her to walk forward.

Dad stopped halfway in, and halfway out, of the pew and glared at me. I sighed.

Seriously? He was going to do this now with everyone and their brother watching us?

The anger must've shown on my face, which was easily read, causing him to turn his back on me and start striding toward the door, not bothering to acknowledge the funeral workers at the door trying to tell us where to go.

Abel, Marnie, Verity and I listened, however, and walked to where he'd directed us—which was to the family limousine.

I noticed Eugene duck into the car, and I resigned myself for a very unpleasant ride.

Verity caught the movement, and held out her hand.

"I'll get the car and follow directly behind you. Okay?"

Marnie jumped at the chance.

"I'll go with you!"

Marnie knew, just as well as I did, what would happen the moment I dropped down into that car.

Kenneth's mother would start in, and to be honest, I'd rather all of that anger be directed at me rather than at Verity.

Verity, although she'd done nothing wrong, would likely be an easy target, and I didn't want my aunt throwing any bad attitude her way if I could help it.

So yes, I gladly gave her my keys, and pointed at my sister.

"Don't you leave her."

Verity snorted and started walking to my car, using the key to open the door and then fall down inside.

She waved once, and I took a step backward, then turned and got into the limo.

"Well, well, well," my aunt's taunting voice said the moment I got inside. "Look what the cat dragged in."

I gritted my teeth and turned my eyes to gaze out the window.

Only when the seat depressed beside me did I look up to find Abel sitting on the seat next to mine, clearly laying down his allegiance with a single-minded focus.

I would like to think that if I'd been in the right frame of mind, I wouldn't have allowed Verity to ride by herself after all that Beckett had done to the people that were mine. Family. Friends.

Because, had I been in my right mind, I would've driven the two women, and risked the chance of pissing off my aunt.

Because anything beat being in a car and watching the woman you love nearly dying.

***

"What is that?"

I turned in my seat. We'd been driving for a while now, but it was at such a slow pace that I felt confident I could keep Truth's car on the road while I looked.

And my blood turned cold at what I saw.

"Holy shit," I breathed.

There were bikes riding up beside us, and a lot of them.

They passed us, one by one by one until they were riding alongside us, but not overtaking the lead vehicle that held Kenneth's body.

I saw Big Papa, Sean, Aaron, Tommy Tom, and Ghost in a sea of black and red—the Dixie Wardens MC colors—as well as a few of our prospects.

"How sweet," Marnie whispered. "That's a lot of bikers."

"I know that this is way more than is in this particular chapter, so the ones that are here with our boys must be some other bikers that

I've never seen before," I explained. "That's just…"

Something hard hit us.

So hard, in fact, that I jerked the wheel.

Luckily, I managed to go right instead of left, or I would've taken out several bikers in my attempt to keep the car on the road.

My ears were ringing, and my face was stinging.

Then we impacted with something else, and my head hit the steering wheel.

Someone cursed—maybe Marnie—but my head hurt too badly to put much thought into it.

For a few horrifying seconds, I thought I'd lose my lunch, but I managed to hold it down. Had I lost my lunch, my head would've started hurting worse, and that would've sucked because it was already pounding so hard that I worried for the state of my eyeballs.

Surely, if I puked, my eyeballs would pop out of my head. And if that happened, Truth would likely be disgusted and have to leave me out of self-preservation.

The car groaned, causing me to open my eyes.

Bikers surrounded me.

They were everywhere.

One was by my window looking in—the one with a Mohawk. Another was staring at me through the windshield—a windshield that had a large hole through the glass.

Had I hit something? Had a rock done that? God, I sure hoped I didn't wreck Truth's car over a freakin' rock!

The door was pried open, and someone groaned.

It was only after I felt the groan vibrate in my chest a second time that I realized that someone was me.

Something hot dripped down my face, and I reached my hand upward to wipe it off my face, but found my hand unable to cooperate.

The door at my side was yanked open by Mohawk guy, and I blinked at him.

"You're okay," he said in a deep baritone that under any other situation would've sent chills down my spine with how delicious he sounded. This time, though, it only made me smile weakly.

"That's a good girl," he grinned for me. "Do you hurt?"

I tried to speak, swallowed, then tried again.

"My head."

His eyes moved from my own, to something beside my head, and then back to my eyes.

"Yeah," he agreed. "I'm sure it does. Is your hearing okay?"

I licked my lips and tasted copper.

"I don't have blood all over my face, do I?" I asked him.

"Nah," he said. "Not much, anyway."

"You look like Carrie," came Marnie's weak reply. "Oh, hey! I have a sexy man at my door, too!"

I tried to turn, but Mohawk guy's hands were suddenly on my face. "Don't move until we know if you have a neck injury."

"You act like you have medical knowledge or something," I grumbled, resigning myself to the fate of having another man's hands on me. "You're not Truth, you know. You should probably not touch me."

"Yes, ma'am," Mohawk guy ignored me. "Under any other circumstances, I wouldn't be touching you. I'm a happily married man with two children. My paramedic skills don't just turn off, though."

I smiled. "You don't look like a paramedic."

"What do I look like?"

Was he just talking to humor me?

"Like a big ol' teddy bear," I told him. "With a mohawk," I felt obligated to add.

Mohawk guy laughed.

The rich sound was interrupted, though, by something I never wanted to hear again.

Truth's bellow of anger jolted me, and I moved my eyes since Mohawk guy wouldn't let me move my head, and nearly groaned at the panicked look in his eyes at seeing his car.

"I didn't mean to!" I cried out. "I swear! I will fix your car!"

"I'm not sure he's worried about the car, honey. Does your arm hurt?"

I thought about it, then decided that yes, indeed, it did hurt.

Like a mother fucker.

"Yes," I told him. "Should it hurt?"

He didn't reply.

Something shook the car, and I jerked, my eyes going wide as my head reminded me that it wasn't very happy with me.

CHAPTER 21

Whiskey: Because who in the hell needs feelings.

-Life Lesson

Verity

"We got an anonymous tip that this was about to go down," the large older man said as he held out a piece of paper to Truth.

Truth took it, and then turned to stare at me for long seconds before returning the paper.

"What?" I asked.

I was so intimidated.

My hospital bed was surrounded by bikers, and they were guarding me like I was something precious to them.

Something Truth informed me over an hour ago that I was— precious to him. And if I was important to him, I was protected by not just his chapter of The Dixie Wardens MC, but all of the members of The Dixie Wardens MC. All eight chapters, and two thousand three hundred and forty-five members.

Though, only a mere forty-five members were in my hospital room or outside in the hallway.

Anyone would be absolutely stupid to do anything with this many members around. And not because a lot of them were law enforcement, or had been at one point.

But because they were generally scary mother fuckers.

Even Mohawk guy was scary, though he'd introduced himself as Kettle about twenty minutes ago.

I was now sitting in my hospital bed, my face stinging, as my broken arm was being set in a hot pink cast by yet another hunky man—this one Dr. Tommy—listening to the men talk while I valiantly tried to hide the fact that I was fighting off the urge to puke from my still raging headache.

I was also trying to decide if hearing what the men had to say was worth the additional pain that concentrating on their conversation would surely bring.

"You're fucking kidding me," Truth growled. "You tried calling?"

The older man who'd introduced himself as Silas nodded his head. "Yeah, but your phones were off for the funeral. We'd started heading this way around eight this morning to make it in time to see you patch in your prospects later tonight and offer our condolences."

"I guess you heard about the problems we've been having with Elais Beckett?" Big Papa asked from his position down by my feet. His hand was resting on my toes, and every once in a while, he'd squeeze them, then continue listening. It was an absent gesture; one I wasn't sure if he realized he was doing or not.

But I continued to let him because it felt good. I saw Silas nod an affirmative to answer Big Papa's question.

Truth was on my left, his hand playing up and down the length of my arm, reassuring himself that I was okay by touching me and feeling the heat of my skin.

"After you left, we got the call about the funeral and decided to head this way. A ride's a ride," Sebastian, Silas' son and the vice president of the Benton Chapter, said.

I'd heard that by Truth before. Any length of a trip, as long as he got to ride there, was a good thing.

"How'd you hear that we were patching in our prospects tonight?"

Silas smiled.

"I've got my ways." He replied, but we all knew that Silas knows everything. All of our chapters report information to him.

That cryptic message had Big Papa sighing in annoyance, and I looked at him.

His face was haggard, and he looked like he was about to fall over on his feet.

I frowned.

He looked sick.

I wiggled my toes, but the playful gesture costed me as any type of movement—even breathing—made my head want to explode.

The smile that he gave me, although small, was still worth the pain that I felt.

Something that Big Papa noticed when his eyes caught mine.

But before he could say anything, Dr. Tommy Tom, the hunky man, stood up and gave me a light tap on the cheek with two fingers.

"All done. Don't do any strenuous exercise with that hand until the cast comes off and new x-rays are run to be sure that everything has healed up just fine.

"Okay," I sighed in exasperation. There went all my forward progress on my bench presses. "I'll be sure to…"

"What the fuck!"

I winced, both because of what Randi's extremely unhappy screech did to my head, but also because Randi was here, and she was pissed.

Truth's hand squeezed my arm lightly, and I would've squeezed him back were I not hurting.

"Somebody better move so I can see my best friend, or I'm not going to be very nice about this," Randi snapped from somewhere beyond the doorway.

The bikers parted, allowing my friend entrance.

The minute she saw me, she paused, composed herself, and then started forward once again.

"You look like ass," she declared.

I flipped her off, but didn't reply.

"Are you okay? What the hell happened?" she asked, her eyes studying my face.

"She was about two inches from taking a bullet to the face," Truth growled. "How do you think she is?"

I made a feeble effort to smack him on the thigh, causing him to chuckle.

"I'm fine," I told Randi. "My face hurts, and I probably have a small concussion. I have a bruised eardrum, and my arm is broken. Aside from those things, though, I'm doing just great."

Randi just stared at me for a long few moments before turning around and walking right back out the door.

She was gone for a few long seconds before I heard a muffled, angry scream, and then she was right back at my side, her game face in place.

"What do you think of the color?" I asked, holding my arm up.

The medicine that I'd been given for my headache finally started to take effect, and it was slowly beginning to release me from its painful grip.

It sure was easier to think when your head wasn't pounding so hard that your stomach churned.

"I think it's hideous, but you know how I hate pink."

She did hate pink. She didn't own a single pink garment, not a shirt, not a pair of underwear, not socks or workout gear. Pink was my favorite color, though, and I had tons of things in all different shades of it.

I grinned, my face stinging from the multitude of tiny cuts that dotted my face, causing me to wince in response.

"What the hell happened?" she asked, touching her fingers to a point just underneath my eye.

Right underneath the stitches.

"We're going to take this into the hall, baby," Truth rumbled from my side.

I felt his hand in my hair, brushing it away from my face, and then he placed a soft kiss on my cheek—one of the only places that wasn't cut or hurting—and left.

Leaving me to explain to my best friend what exactly had happened.

"So…" I started.

"So…" she snapped.

Oh, man. She was really mad.

"Your friend was shot at and nearly took a bullet to the head," Marnie started off without preamble.

I winced.

I'd been trying to ease gently into that part.

"What?" Randi shrieked. "What the fuck, Verity? Is that true?"

I nodded, my stomach started to roil. It felt like three days ago when I'd woken up with a hangover, only ten times worse.

"Yes," I sighed. "And no, I don't know what's going on. That was what the big bad biker meeting was when you came in. Apparently, the sexy older man who was standing just inside the doorway when you entered heard about it and tried to intercept us before anything could happen, but they were a few minutes too late. Just as they were pulling alongside of us in the funeral procession, some sniper took a shot at me – right through the windshield! They're fairly convinced that the sniper was after Truth, and not me. It was just bad luck that I was the one driving his car."

"Verity…" Randi said. "I don't even know what to say."

I shrugged and immediately regretted it.

"I don't either," I admitted, trying to find a comfortable position that didn't take much movement on my part. I finally settled with my knee half bent, and my head lolling against the white railing that was attached to the bed. "I'm just as in the dark and confused as you are."

"The sound of the bullet coming through the glass and hitting the seat next to her head made her jerk the wheel, causing her to overcorrect and slam into a dumpster filled with cinder blocks on the side of the ride at this construction site we happened to be passing. The impact shattered her arm, and her head hit the steering wheel. Her right ear drum is bruised, and could possibly burst, so they're keeping a close eye on it." Marnie kept going, "She has a concussion, some contusions on her face from the glass when the windshield shattered, and stitches under her right eye from what they think was some glass that got trapped between her face and the steering wheel when she smacked her head on it."

Randi looked at the cut under my eye.

"Did the doctor say you would have scars?"

My eyes drifted closed. "He said he could have a plastic surgeon look at it," I yawned. "I haven't decided if I'm going to do it yet."

"You're doing it."

That was Truth.

I let my eyes open to slits and stared at him.

"What makes you think so?" I challenged.

I watched his eyes flare as a flash of pleasure started to rise inside of me.

He'd been devastated at seeing me hurt, and he hadn't smiled all night. I could see the relief in his eyes that my challenging him caused. Seeing me act like my normal, difficult self was obviously alleviating at least some of his worry.

"Because if I have to look at that scar for the rest of my life, I'm going to murder Elais Beckett in cold blood, then re-fucking-vive him and do it all over again. I might take nursing classes just so I can keep him alive." His smile was mean. "I've got basic field trauma training, but not what I'd need to be able to kill and resuscitate him on daily basis while also keeping him alive during subsequent murder attempts."

I blinked.

Randi snickered.

Marnie sighed and got up.

"You need to see someone about all that pent-up anger," she said. "Have you heard from Dad?"

Truth's eyes narrowed on his sister.

"He's in the waiting room," he answered. "He's been asking for you. Abel's been kind enough to deal with him so I didn't have to."

Abel had been in and out of here a few times, but he kept disappearing. Now I knew why.

"I'll go talk to him. Maybe he'll go away," Marnie grunted a word I couldn't quite hear, and disappeared into the sea of bikers I could still see through my hospital room door.

That left Randi, me and Truth alone, and I didn't have to wait long for the fireworks to continue.

"So what are you going to do about this shit, Truth?" Randi snapped. "You're not protecting her. In fact, if I had to say anything about your job so far, I'd give you a big fat *F*."

I groaned.

"Randi, you're not helping," I murmured softly. "Please, just let us…or them…fix this. Figure it out. I'm going to do whatever the hell they tell me to do, and if that's stay inside for the next three months and eat ice cream all day long, then I'm going to do it."

Truth's hand found my cheek—the only spot that didn't have a cut on it—causing me to open my eyes and stare at him.

"What?" my voice cracked.

"I'm not going to make you stay inside for three months and eat ice cream all day…but you're going to be heavily guarded, and I rented a car for you to use. And you'll also be shadowed by someone you haven't met yet."

"Who is it?" I asked warily.

He smiled.

"His name is Rafe, and he was trained by one of my grandpa's best men."

That brought a thought to the forefront of my mind.

"When you took me to your grandpa's pub for the first time, there was this man in black."

"Ronan," he answered instantly. "He's an...enforcer."

"An enforcer of what?" I asked.

"Justice."

"And is this same man that trained Rafe?" I put voice to my suspicion.

Truth's mouth grinning, and I could tell I wouldn't like the answer.

"Ronan trained a lot of people, but yes, he trained Rafe as well."

"He trained you, too, didn't he?"

Truth nodded.

"Who is he an enforcer for?"

I didn't know why I was pushing this. I hadn't broached this subject because I could sense that it was a tough one for him. Something he hadn't wanted me to know.

But I was pushing it, and I felt like there was more to the story...something more that I hadn't quite caught on to yet.

He looked over at Randi, and she silently left, somehow sensing that there was something more to the story here, and that she didn't want to stop the flow of data that Truth was willing to share.

And I was grateful.

"A long time ago, my pop was a part of an organization."

That was all he said, and I growled in frustration.

"Truth..."

He grinned.

"Pop was part of a club of Irish bikers, a club that originated out of

Ireland. When he moved here with my grandmother, he left that all behind…but Ronan decided to come with him. He, for some reason, thought he owed my grandfather a debt for saving him when he was a young teen, and never left him. Ronan was my grandfather's best friend. He raised my mother right alongside my grandparents. There's literally nothing that Ronan wouldn't do for my grandfather."

"Where is Ronan?" I asked, a thought dawning as he started to explain.

Truth grimaced.

"Ronan's looking for Beckett."

My eyes widened.

"Is he going to kill him?" I asked hoarsely.

Truth shrugged.

"Honestly?" He stood up and ran his fingers through his hair. "I don't give a flying fuck if he does. As long as he's not around to bother you, harass you, or put you—or anyone else I know—in danger any more, I don't give a shit what happens to him. Sure, I'd rather him suffer the rest of his days in prison—I know enough cops, wardens and security guards to make his life inside a living hell—but at this point, I just want to be rid of him, and I'd do damn near anything for it."

The words, although harsh, made my heart swell.

This was going to be bad, I just knew it. But I couldn't find it in me to care at that moment in time. Truth was here, his hand resting gently on my head, and my headache was dissipating.

And with the headache no longer hammering out a staccato in my brain, I found myself extremely tired.

"You pressed my button," I accused.

Truth didn't even look the least bit sorry.

"You need to rest."

"I need to talk to you," I countered.

My eyes were drifting closed of their own volition, but the moment his mouth pressed against mine, they peeled open.

"Thank you."

"For what?" he whispered, pushing back a stray strand of hair.

"For loving me."

"How do you know I love you?" His grin was warm.

I lifted my good hand—the one that wasn't throbbing in time with the beat of my heart—and placed it on his cheek.

"I saw your face today," I told him.

His grin disappeared.

"Only a man who loves a woman looks that devastated at the sight you saw today."

I didn't actually see what he saw, but I could imagine.

At first, I'd thought his dismay had been about the car, but I quickly realized differently the moment he bellowed my name.

And when his hand touched mine, I knew that I loved him just as much as he loved me.

And even now, I could see the love shining in his eyes.

"I love you back, you know," I told him. "Have for a while now."

He placed a single kiss on the tip of my nose, and I let my eyes fall closed once again.

Then I was dead to the world and missing all the good stuff.

Lani Lynn Vale

CHAPTER 22

*'Cause Satan told me so isn't a good excuse
when you have to explain to your partner why
you did something.*

-Fact of Life

Truth

The moment she fell asleep, I studied her face, wondering if I was making the wrong decision by staying with her.

I was fairly sure, however, that it wouldn't matter if I left her for her protection at this point. Elais Beckett knew what she meant to me, and he'd do whatever he had to do to kill her.

He may have missed her today, but he'd gotten me anyway. He now knew my weakness, and I'd given that to him without even realizing I'd done it.

I'd been in the middle of an argument with my aunt, cousin, and father when I'd seen my car careen past us out of the corner of my eye.

I'd turned just in time to see my car— with my sister and my woman inside—hit the dumpster.

My scream of agony had forced the limo driver to pull over, and the moment we'd slowed enough for me to bail out, I had.

I'd sprinted toward the car, my heart in my throat.

By the time I'd finally arrived, my car had been surrounded.

My sister had been standing beside the wrecked car, a small cut on her forehead from what I assumed was glass.

Knowing instinctively that she was okay, I'd turned my attention to my woman, only to see a bullet hole through the windshield where her face would be.

Kettle had been leaning into the car, his big body blocking my view; I hadn't realized that she was okay at the time I'd called her name.

Agony and heartache had laced my words, and I knew everyone around me could tell how much she'd meant to me in that moment.

And then Kettle had moved and I'd seen her.

I'd seen the blood on her face.

I'd seen the agony etched over her face as pain tore through her.

What I hadn't seen, thank God, was a bullet hole.

The next two hours had been a blur of activity as my fellow Dixie Wardens had rallied around me, making sure that my woman had all the care that she could and would need.

Now, here I sat, finally watching her sleep peacefully, wondering if I was doing the right thing.

"You're doing the right thing."

I looked up to find Ghost standing there.

"How do you know?" I asked, my voice thick with what I realized were tears.

I hadn't cried in five years—since I'd found out that I'd killed not just one innocent, but many innocents—and I realized that this was way worse than that.

Sure, I'd fucked up by putting those men down years ago, and I would always live with that black mark on my soul.

But this, knowing that I'd put Verity in the crosshairs of a madman over something I'd done was enough to kill me.

"Because if you were wrong, if your decision was wrong, you wouldn't be wondering if you were doing the right thing," he explained. "If there was one thing I could wish for right now, it'd be to have my life back. To rewind to five years ago when my daughter was a baby, and my wife had no clue what kind of a man she'd married."

Twelve hours ago, had he said this, my curiosity would've been piqued. Now, with Verity lying so still in the hospital bed, I realized that I didn't care about anyone but her. And that likely made me an ass, but I literally couldn't deal with anyone else's shit. I could barely deal with my own.

"She could die," I said bluntly. "What do I do if she does die?"

"She won't," he said. "There are eighteen Dixie Wardens in this hospital ward, and four about half a day from being patched in. They all, along with me, have your woman's safety at heart. They won't—I won't—let anything happen to her. I swear to Christ."

His sincerity made my heart relax minutely, and I closed my eyes and leaned my head down, letting my forehead fall down to come to a rest next to Verity's hand. The same hand that was now broken.

Fucking Beckett.

"Don't make the same mistake as me, man," Ghost said to my lowered head. "Take it from me. I've regretted it every day for eighteen hundred and fifty-two days. And I've watched her find a man last week. My heart's in fucking shreds right now, but I made my bed. Make sure you don't make yours, too."

With that he left, and the door closed softly behind him with a whispered click.

My eyes squeezed tightly closed before I got up, placed a single kiss on her face, and walked out of the room.

Ghost was right.

I wasn't going to give her up. Not now, not ever.

And as I sat down in a chair in a hospital waiting room with The Dixie Wardens at my sides, I realized three things.

One, I had a great group of men at my back.

Two, Elais Beckett was a dead man.

Three, I should've never doubted the severity of Ronan's anger.

***

Four hours later

"You're sure this is it?" I asked. "How do you have this information so fast?"

I was standing about a hundred yards from a hotel room that Silas had found two towns over. There was a man that fit the last known description of Elais Beckett who was seen going into this hotel room with another male in his late sixties.

"Silas has so many fucking secrets that he could fill a goddamned water tower full of them. Just be happy he found the information, and whatever you do, don't ask questions about how or what he had to do to get that information."

That was Big Papa, reprimanding me like I was some misbehaving child.

I ignored him and turned my attention back to the hotel room.

"A man called me. He said he was a friend of yours," Silas said. "Said his name was 'Ro.'"

He'd told me that before, and I didn't really know a 'Ro.' I did, however, know a Ronan.

"If that's Ronan, my grandfather's man, in there, we can't go in there with guns blazing because he might retaliate before he realizes that it's us," I said. "I've tried calling him four times now. Either he has his phone off, or he's ignoring my call."

It was more likely that he was ignoring my call. He never had his phone off due to the fact that he had a daughter who he loved with all his heart, and if she called, he would drop everything—even Elais Beckett—and go to her.

Though, she hadn't called him in over two years. They'd had a falling out about his behavior and his way of life, and she'd written him off.

That didn't mean that he didn't wait for her call.

"Tried the hotel room phone yet?" Aaron asked.

"What the hell are y'all even doing here?" I asked. "Y'all could lose your jobs."

Aaron and Big Papa looked at me like I was crazy.

"Right now, we're Dixie Wardens, not police officers," Big Papa finally explained. "And you're not getting rid of us. Stop your bitching and moaning and get in there. I have to be at work in four hours."

Alrighty, then.

That was exactly what I did.

I walked up to the door, knocked and was unsurprised when Ronan answered the door.

"About time you got here," he grumbled. "I had to practically draw you a fuckin' map."

I turned to find Silas, Kettle, Sean, Aaron, Big Papa, Ghost, and Sebastian at my back, staring at the man that'd help raise me with about as much worry as I had on my face.

233

"Well, I'm here now," I said. "What do you have for me?"

Ronan stepped back, opened the door wide, and we all froze, our eyes uncomprehending at what, exactly, we were seeing.

Then Big Papa groaned.

"There's a time and place for things like that, and that's on Halloween, or a fucking big screen," someone else added.

Sean, I thought.

"You're a paramedic, right?"

Sean grunted and pushed past us into the room, stopping beside the bed where Elais Beckett was tied down on.

"How did you do this all without attracting the attention of the cops?" I asked, horror lacing my words.

Ronan had always been inventive when it came to his punishments when I was younger, but had I known that he was capable of this, I might've been way more scared of him than I was.

"Jesus Christ."

That was Silas, who came to stand beside me, looking down on the bed with so much awe and a fair bit of disgust that he wasn't sure which emotion to feel.

"Do you think he cries more when his dick is pulled, or when his tongue is?" Ghost rumbled from my other side.

It was a good question.

Not only was Beckett tied by his ankles and wrists to fucking eye bolts, Ronan had drilled into the hotel's freakin' walls, but he was also attached to the ceiling by a rope.

Both of them were threaded through his body parts like a goddamned fish.

Ronan had cut a hole, likely with his own pocket knife, into both appendages, and then threaded a piece of braided brown, abrasive twine through each hole and then tied it into a knot. Then he'd attached it to another eye bolt that hung from the ceiling.

His eyes were wild, and he was crying.

But I couldn't find a goddamned reason in the world to feel sorry for him.

"Beckett?" I said to him when his gaze caught mine. His eyes widened, and I said two words. "Check mate."

The blood pooling under Beckett's body was drawing my eyes, and I finally pulled the plug on the horror show.

"Get him an ambulance, Sean," I ordered. "We can't have him dying on us. Plus, I'd like to make sure his life isn't as easy as dying would be."

Sean disappeared out of the hotel room, and it didn't take long for the sirens to be heard.

I waited there, long after the other men left the room to avoid being seen, and watched as paramedics, cops, and firefighters arrived on scene.

All of whom I knew personally.

"Whoa," said a large, muscular, African-American police officer who went by the name of Tough. He was the nicest man I'd ever had the pleasure of working with…until you pissed him off. Then he was meanest, most vindictive man you would ever have the displeasure of meeting.

It was something that luckily didn't happen very often, and I'd never been on the receiving end of it, thank God.

I'd seen him go off on one of his best friends once when said friend had made an offensive comment about his woman. His woman was a tiny Asian girl with the prettiest brown eyes I'd ever seen and about half of Tough's height. Tough felt the need to protect her as if she couldn't easily take care of herself. God help you if you made a derogatory comment toward her.

"What the hell is that through his dick?"

That was from another officer, McClain.

"From what I can tell, it's twine," I finally said once the men got a closer look.

"Back away, please," a haughty paramedic/firefighter ordered in a low, husky voice.

I turned and shuffled to get out of the woman's way, and wondered if she saw the way the other firefighters looked at her.

They were staring at her like she was an incompetent newbie who was about to get wigged out over the gory state of Elais Beckett's body.

But much to my surprise, and the other firefighters, the little woman went right up to the bloody mass that was Beckett and started working on him instantly.

My brows went up at the nearest firefighter, and he mouthed a 'later' at me before waving me out of his way.

I moved completely out of the room, unsurprised when McClain and Tough followed me out.

"What in the goat fuck was that?" Tough asked in derision.

"That," I said slowly. "Was the man who took a shot at my woman with a sniper rifle this morning while she was driving my car and missed her head by two inches."

Tough's eyes widened.

"*You* did that?"

I shook my head, about to reply, when Big Papa sidled up to one side, and Aaron moved up on the other.

"We got an anonymous tip that he was here," Big Papa rumbled.

That was partially the truth, right? Giving up the man responsible away would be cruel and unusual punishment.

I knew for certain that they weren't going to give Ronan up…or weren't going to until Ronan turned himself in.

"I was the one who did it," Ronan said.

We all turned to find him standing behind our small group huddle, and Tough tilted his head to the side.

"You did *what*?" Tough asked.

It wasn't every day that a man came up to you and admitted to the gruesome torture of someone.

"You heard me correctly," Ronan confirmed. "Now, arrest me before I try to run."

He looked like the kind of person that wouldn't, and didn't run. He was big, blocky, and in dress shoes. There was no way in hell he would get away from Tough on a bad day, let alone a good one.

Ronan wouldn't try. He knew how to read people just like I did.

Tough, however, was still confused.

"You're saying that you did all that?"

Ronan, upon first glance, didn't ever strike anyone as the type of man who would do anything violent. He looked like a fuckin' teddy bear and was always smiling.

It was the smile that got you. It'd gotten me quite a few times.

I'd never known he was mad until he'd struck.

"I'm saying that that little fucker killed my best friend," Ronan said with his Irish lilt thickening. "I'm also saying that I killed him for killing my friend and his wife. I have a tape of the confession. Though, that came first. The rest came after he admitted all the awful things he's done since he was released early from prison."

Tough pulled out a set of handcuffs.

"Well then, I suppose it's my duty to take you into the station and get this sorted out."

With that, Tough led a handcuffed Ronan away, leaving me standing in the middle of chaos wondering if I was lucky enough for it all to be over.

Ronan stopped about halfway to the car, and turned.

Tough, not really thinking correctly at the moment, let him.

"The gun he used to shoot your woman is in the trunk of the car over there," he nodded his head in the direction of a black sedan about halfway across the small parking lot. "And I found the spent shell casing, too."

Exhilaration filled me.

"Thanks, Ronan," I called to him.

He winked, causing my heart to warm.

My grandfather and grandmother, and I supposed Kenneth, now had retribution.

I hadn't wanted them to die, but now we'd at least have attempted murder pinned on the man responsible.

The rest would soon follow.

CHAPTER 23

You know that moment when you close a cabinet door and you hear something fall? Yeah, that's someone else's problem.

-Fact of Life

Truth

Two hours later at the same hospital that Verity was in, I had a throw down with my president.

"I need fifteen minutes with him," I argued with Big Papa and Aaron. "I won't hurt him."

"You better not," Big Papa grumbled as he pushed up from his chair beside Beckett's hospital bed. A bed that he was handcuffed to—at the wrists and ankles—a nearly similar situation to the one I'd found him in only two hours before. Though they'd left his dick and tongue alone.

Apparently, those weren't the usual restraint methods that the hospital employed.

Aaron left, too. But only after receiving permission from me to leave Tank in Verity's room while he ran up the road to have lunch with his wife.

Since he didn't like leaving Tank in the car, and they were going into a semi-fancy restaurant, he'd decided it might be easier to leave Tank here.

"Don't forget to give him water when you finally get back to Verity's room," Aaron said as he left.

I tipped an imaginary hat at him and turned back to the bed.

Beckett was awake and staring at me like one would a large pile of dog shit.

"What?" I asked, a smile overtaking my face. "Was there something that you wanted to talk about?"

He sneered.

"Tell me why," I ordered.

Beckett smiled, and it took everything I had not to laugh at how ridiculous he sounded with a newly pierced hole in his tongue. "Why would I?"

That was followed up by a leer, and I clenched my fists tightly and bared my teeth.

I wanted to punch that smile off his face, but refrained. Barely.

The only thing keeping me in check was the promise I'd made to my president, after all.

"Because you're not a coward. You're an asshole, and a piece of shit, but you don't run from shit like this. That would make you no better than a rodent…and we all know how much you hate being compared to rats."

Beckett was phobic of rats. If there was one thing in this world that he was afraid of, rats were it. Something I'd be utilizing seeing as he was going to be spending a damn fair amount of time in the state penitentiary.

Though, he'd done that himself when he'd picked up that rifle and taken a shot at my woman. See, his bail prevented him from obtaining firearms, which was only a minor offense compared to his other offenses.

Like, oh…murder and attempted murder.

Unlucky for him, he'd left evidence behind, and now we had the weapon used in the attempted murder of my wife.

"Come on," I cajoled. "Why don't you just tell me for old time's sake. Then we can reminisce on how much I hate you after you're done explaining."

Beckett turned his fat head away from me, causing a smile to overtake my mouth.

"Okay," I said cheerfully. "The hard way it is."

I walked over to his medicine pump that was feeding pain relief into his veins to keep him comfortable and started pressing buttons.

When I was sure it'd stopped sending the good stuff into his veins, I took a seat, pulled my phone out of my pocket and started reading the latest Jim Butcher book.

I'd read it over five times since it'd come out, so I wasn't worried about stopping at a good part when he finally decided to start talking.

And I didn't worry that he would. He was probably in some serious pain, and it wouldn't be long before that pain would ramp back up on him.

I just had to sit here and wait.

***

It took him forty-five minutes.

The first indication that anything was wrong was the red that crept up his face to settle in his cheekbones, followed shortly by the tears.

The tears were my favorite part.

I nearly pulled my phone's camera app up to take a picture, but I figured that would be pushing it.

"Fine!" he screamed.

My brows rose as I looked at him over my shoulder.

"You're ready to talk?" I asked.

His grimace was obvious.

"Fix my pain meds, and I'll tell you anything you want to know," he ordered thickly, his words rolling together as he spoke.

"Dick hurt?" I asked, pocketing my phone and standing up.

His refusal to answer was answer enough.

Grinning, I reached for the pillow that was behind his head, and yanked.

The jolt sent his body forward, and an audible groan left his mouth seconds later.

"No!" he sounded like he had a mouthful of cotton.

Grinning at him a tad bit manically, I placed the pillow down onto his crotch and started to put pressure down on it.

He squealed.

"Ready?"

He nodded jerkily, tears now coursing down his face uncontrollably.

"Okay then," I left the pillow there and sat back down. "Enlighten me."

He swallowed, then started to speak. I had to really concentrate to hear his words, but in the end, I got the gist.

"Your grandfather, my best friend, ruined me. Ruined my life," he hiccupped. "It all started with him stealing your grandmother—my

242

fiancé—out from under my nose while I was off fighting in the war."

My eyes closed as a wave of nausea rolled over me.

"Then, throughout the years, he continued to take from me. I ruled these streets, and the whole fucking city, with an iron fist," he snapped. "And slowly, ever so fucking slowly, he continued to take until I had no more income left. Yet, I still let him have his way. 'Oh, Beck. You need to be a good man,' the old bastard used to say to me. And then he gave me you…and then you ruined my operation."

I had.

The moment I'd realized exactly what was going on, I'd contacted a few people who knew how to handle this kind of an operation, and they set about dismantling Beckett's business, which apparently had ruined his business for a *second* time.

First my grandfather had done it by refusing to make the townspeople pay protection fees by offering them his own protection and then I'd taken away his other source of income.

He must have thought that we had set out to make that happen, but he couldn't be more wrong. My grandfather had never, not one single time, spoken a harsh word about Elais Beckett. It'd been me who turned him in to the cops. It'd been me who'd dismantled his operation, and it'd been me who'd had my computer man, Jack, hack into Beckett's account and deliver ten million dollars to the man's family that I'd killed.

Had I had it in me to give, I'd have given it to him.

I hadn't realized, at the time, that the man was mentally unstable. Had no clue that he'd been a vet with severe PTSD who was hellbent on going out in a blaze of cop assisted suicide. He got me instead.

But that could've been me, coming back from deployment only to have bigger, emotional battles at home. So it was almost like shooting myself the day I found out all the things that'd been plaguing that poor man.

The man that I'd shot during the rescue of a small child who I was told he had kidnapped.

"Anything else you'd like to tell me?" I asked. "If you give it to me now, I won't take it from you later."

He must've understood my sincerity, because by the time he was done speaking, thirty minutes later, I'd gotten not just the confession of my grandfather, grandmother, and cousin's murder, but also the attempted murder on Verity, and how he'd planned the whole thing.

I was spitting mad, but I left him there, almost the same way I had found him, and barely made it to the bathroom in time to lose my lunch.

Lucky for me, Big Papa hadn't gone too far, and he'd heard the entire thing. Something he told me five minutes later when I finally emerged from the bathroom.

"You did good," he said. "I'm happy that you didn't try to kill him."

I wasn't.

But I also wasn't a killer…at least not anymore.

That didn't mean that I didn't want to go in there and skin him alive with my bare hands.

"Do you mind watching over Verity for a few minutes while I go home, change, and feed the cat?

The cat that I'd forgotten about in the last couple of hours.

I'd called my neighbor and told her not to bother going over today because we'd be back by nightfall. But that was before Verity's head had nearly been blown apart, and I'd forgotten about everything but her.

Big Papa nodded.

"Yeah, I can do that," he said, offering me his hand. "Maybe grab some food while you're out."

Was I hungry?

Yes. Yes, I was.

Would I eat?

No, probably not.

I nodded at Big Papa anyway, though. What he didn't know, wouldn't hurt him.

CHAPTER 24

I'll never, ever let you go.

-Verity talking to her dessert

Verity

A dog's barking woke me up.

One second I was in dreamland, and the next I was staring at a man across the room, wielding a syringe in one hand and an IV pole in the other.

He was swinging it at the dog—Aaron's K-9, Tank—and trying to keep the dog at bay.

He was failing miserably.

I started to stand, but froze when something in my leg started to pinch.

I looked down at the large syringe sticking out of my thigh, and wondered what the hell it was doing there.

I pulled it out of my leg, my heart starting to pound.

Sweat popped out on my forehead, and my stomach roiled. All over a single syringe in my thigh.

Nice, Verity, very nice.

I swung my legs over the bed, my intent to get to Tank and stop the man from hitting him again, but the moment my feet hit the cool tiled floor, my legs went out from under me.

I hit the floor with a thud, and my head and arm screamed.

Not that my head wasn't already screaming, because it was. Loud, booming and seriously pissed off.

I got my legs underneath me, my hand going to my forehead to try to counteract the steady pounding of my head, and moaned.

The dog's whimper had me glancing up sharply, and it took everything I had not to start crying in pain.

I didn't make a sound, though, knowing that if I could just somehow help Tank, he would take it from there.

The night Truth had fed me nothing but cookies for dinner, I witnessed the power in Tank's body as he'd taken the padded man—who just so happened to have been Truth, something I hadn't known at the time—and forced him to sit still as he'd waited for Aaron to call him off.

The fury in his barks now, compared to then, were much different.

It seemed like Tank knew that this man was a real threat to me, and he was going to protect me with his life.

Maybe if I could trip the man with my prone body…

Alarms started to go off, and I heard a worried voice say 'Code Brown!' over the loudspeaker, and I would've laughed at the use of 'Code Brown' had this situation not been extremely fucked up as it was.

"Tank," my voice cracked when the dog went down to his haunches.

Tank didn't spare me a glance as he did some amazing roll thing and went for the man's knee.

My eyes took in the man as he went down to drop his weight on the dog, and it was then that I realized that this man was dressed in a hospital gown with handcuffs dangling from his wrists.

His feet, which were bloody as well, slipped.

He came down hard on top of Tank, and I heard the distinct sound of something breaking.

Oh, God. Please don't let that be Tank's bones! I chanted to myself as I crawled another inch.

My heart was racing. My vision was blurry now, and I couldn't control my breaths.

I knew without a shadow of a doubt that the man had stabbed me with that syringe. And that something bad had been in that syringe, and was now racing through my bloodstream.

Saliva filled my mouth, and I took one last ditch effort to get to Tank…and failed.

***

Ghost

My heart was broken. My skin was tight. My eyes hurt. My head was pounding.

Though, I couldn't tell which was physical or emotional, I knew that I couldn't go on like this any longer.

Something had to give.

I knew as I walked into the hospital, rage filling my veins, that I had to find a way out of this mess that I found myself in.

"Code brown, second floor."

I stopped as two doctors, three nurses, and a stumbling Big Papa ran in the direction of the stairs.

I hurried in the direction, my head no longer pounding as adrenaline poured through me. All my aches and pains were null and void as I took the stairs two at a time, surpassing Big Papa who was bleeding from a head wound.

He moved over, letting me pass, and I caught up to the last nurse.

I overtook her, too, and hit the second-floor landing and yanked the large metal door open before following the last nurse and doctor.

They were all standing outside of a room—Verity's room—and staring in like they didn't know what to do.

I could hear Tank snarling, and in between snarls were pained whimpers that he was trying very hard to contain.

"Move," I barked out, pushing my way past the nurses and doctors gathered around the entrance.

They moved, and I almost wished they hadn't.

Because on the floor was a nightmare.

Blood was…everywhere.

On the bed, on the floor, on the walls. If you had any imagination at all, this was worse.

A man lay dead, his throat torn out, on the floor.

Elais Beckett.

I could just see the edge of Verity's hair as it lay fanned out on the floor, the last three quarters of an inch slowly becoming saturated with the blood that was pooling on the floor.

Her face was stark white, and small dots of perspiration were coating it.

And then there was Tank.

His left hind leg was hanging limply, and his eyes were wild as he tried to stay upright.

He had blood on him, too, but I couldn't figure out if it was his or not.

I took a step forward, and Tank's head snapped up.

His growl became deeper, and I realized that Tank wasn't all the way home at the moment.

"Help me."

Those whispered words had me trying to take another step, but Tank took a threatening step forward. Protecting his charge like he was told to do.

"Fuck," I grated. "Big Papa…"

"Shit," Big Papa said as he made his way up to my side.

He looked worse up close than he did far away, and I realized then that what I thought was just a cut was a goddamn gunshot.

"You're about to fall over," I said. "And you got shot in the head."

Big Papa shrugged.

And that was when Truth arrived.

"Verity!"

Truth's scream was heart-wrenching as he ran toward us.

"Truth…" I started to say, trying to grab his hand.

He shook me off and barreled into the room.

Tank went nuts.

Truth backed away, a look of horror on his face as he saw all the blood and Verity lying on the floor.

"Take him out!"

I pulled my gun free of its holster.

"He's hurt, and not thinking straight. You're not killing him," Big Papa was bellowing at the top of his lungs.

"She's dying!" Truth screamed.

My heart hurt.

But I knew, if I had to kill Tank, I wouldn't feel bad about it. At least not until afterwards. Not when it came to Verity's life.

"Find Aaron!" Big Papa bellowed. "He's the only one who's going to call him off."

I pulled my phone out with my free hand and dialed Aaron's number.

"Hello?" Aaron answered.

"Where are you?" I barked.

"I'm right here…what's going on?"

I breathed a sigh of relief when Aaron rounded the corner, a to-go drink from Chili's in his hand.

He saw all of us waiting outside, his brows furrowed, and then he rounded the corner and saw what the wall was hiding from him.

Truth tried to take another step toward Verity, and Tank launched.

"Tank!" Aaron shouted. "Platz!"

Tank fell to his haunches, then rolled over all in one move.

His head fell to the ground, and he started to whine.

Truth launched himself over the dog, gathering Verity into his arms.

The doctors, nurses, and other hospital personnel rushed in as well.

And then everything went to shit.

The dog died. Verity died. Beckett died.

Everyone fucking died.

***

Truth

252

Something heavy fell from the bed that they—at least ten nurses and doctors—were standing around.

I let my eyes fall to the floor.

Bloody footprints were everywhere.

Nurses were slipping in it. One nurse in particular was covered from ass to ankle from when she'd slipped, fallen and gotten up.

Verity was clinically dead. That's what the doctor told me, anyway.

"Get him out of here!"

The same doctor that told me she was dead also kicked me out of the hospital room.

They were doing chest compressions on Verity's small body, and each pump of the doctor's arm I could hear her ribs breaking.

They weren't even in a room. They weren't down in the ER.

They were in the fucking hallway right outside of the room where her life had been stolen from her and snuffed out right before my eyes.

My hands were numb. My brain was, too.

The only thing I could feel was the gaping hole in my chest.

"Everyone clear!"

Every single person moved away from the gurney, and the man wielding the paddles—ones I'd seen many times throughout my years of combat— placed them on Verity's bare chest as I watched helplessly.

The moment her tiny naked body jolted off the bed, I lost it.

I moved to run, but before I could take a step, I was pulled into Big Papa's arms as they encircled me in a bear hug. He held tight and yanked me back.

"Cover her!" I screamed.

Everyone was looking at her, vulnerable and broken, and they didn't even care.

The nurses. Doctors. Techs. Fuck, every single one of the members of my club. People that were in the hospital rooms on either sides of Verity. Everyone was there, watching her, seeing everything.

My eyes were filled with grit and tears, and I strained to get away.

I would've accomplished it, too, but one set of arms became two, and then those two became four.

I was being forced back. Inch by impossible inch.

My body strained to get to Verity. But the harder I tried, the stronger my brothers held on to move me further out of the way.

Then, there was nothing left to see because I was moved into an empty room where we all landed on the floor in a heap.

Big Papa, Sean, and the two prospects—Fender and Jessie James—followed me down.

"Get the fuck off me!" I bellowed, huffing and puffing as I tried in vain to get away from the men.

I knew I wasn't in my right mind.

They knew it, too.

I fought harder, I had to get away.

They couldn't see me like this…not with my heart broken. My pain threatening to spill over from my eyes.

"Get off!" I repeated, swinging blindly.

My fist connected with Sean's face, and the momentum of my punch caused him slide across the floor. His angry eyes full of pain met mine as I winced when I saw his jaw hanging limply, clearly not where it was supposed to be.

His hand went to his face, and then he scrambled across the floor toward me.

Once he was within reach, he returned the punch.

I, at least, took it to the eye instead of to the jaw like he'd done.

Fortunately, when the pain exploded behind my left eye, it didn't break anything pivotal.

I doubled over in pain, grunting as I tried to get to my knees but the weight of the other men who were struggling to contain my rage held me back.

"Get off," I rasped.

I kicked, punched, and genuinely attacked until I had nothing left in me to attack with. All my energy was gone as the adrenaline left my system and I began to crash.

With one final, exhausted huff of breath, I collapsed and let the pain wash over me.

"Jesus fucking Christ," Sean grunted as he moved to place his entire body on one of my arms, all the while he tried not to move his jaw that was most certainly broken.

The others moved, too.

Off of me, unlike Sean. Though, I didn't think that was because he wanted to stay there. More because he *couldn't* move.

Unfortunately for him, he'd given me an easy target. And I felt apologetic as soon as I'd reacted.

"Truth?"

My heart, already shattered, broke even more.

Because standing in the doorway in front of me was Verity's grandmother. She was looking at me with horror written all over her face.

I was bloody. I probably looked wild and broken, but that didn't stop her. No, not Verity's grandmother.

"I'm so sorry," my voice cracked as I climbed to my feet.

Ilsa ran to me, threw her arms around my blood-stained chest, and pressed her frail body into my much larger frame.

***

One hour later

"There's nothing left to do but wait," the doctor said gently.

He knew he was talking to a man on the edge. Someone that was on the verge of going fucking crazy. Someone who'd already torn up one room in this hospital.

Someone who clearly made him very wary, which explained the two security guards and two police officers that were at his back.

He was scared of me. Though, I'd given him reason to be.

"I don't…"

"We're going to have to ask you to leave," the doctor said. "I'll call you periodically, throughout the night, but after what happened here this afternoon… well, hospital policy is clear. We can't allow you to stay."

My heart literally sank.

"But…" I started to say.

Tough and McClain started forward, and I got the drift very quickly.

"Take care of her," I ordered Big Papa, gesturing toward Ilsa.

Though, I needn't have bothered. Ilsa was being looked after by Dixie, of all people. Dixie, a large, older man with a shock of white hair and a matching beard that nearly came all the way down to his chest. He was a member of the Dixie Wardens MC, Benton,

Louisiana Chapter. He was one of the funniest guys I knew, and I had not one single worry that he wouldn't take good care of Verity's GG while I couldn't be there with her.

Big Papa nodded and followed me down, Tough and McClain at his side right along with me.

I walked stiffly over to my bike, through the sea of bikers that were still hanging around and mounted it.

When Big Papa went to follow suit, I held up my hand.

"I need some time," I said gruffly, leaning sideways slightly to kick the stand up.

Big Papa stopped, turned, and studied me.

"I'll come check on you in a few hours."

I didn't bother to reply. I just got on my bike and rode to the only place that felt like her.

Home.

Two hours later, I found myself in the middle of my workshop.

I couldn't breathe.

Everything was closing in on me, and I could do nothing but stand there in the midst of everything that Verity loved, and...*break*.

And I did...completely.

So thoroughly, in fact, that I wasn't sure how many hours had passed as I did so.

The ring of my phone was what broke me out of my thoughts.

I hurried to answer the phone, not caring enough to look to see who it was before I yanked it up and slammed it against my ear.

"How is she?"

"She's stable...ish," Big Papa sounded so tired. Not as tired as I felt, though. "I called about Tank. He made it through surgery. Has a broken hind leg and a few cracked ribs. They expect him to make a full recovery."

Was it bad that I didn't care?

I should. If it wasn't for him, who knows if we would've found her in time.

But I couldn't find it in me to scrounge up the urge to give a shit.

Not when my woman had nearly been killed right before my eyes—twice on the same fucking day.

Right in front of my eyes!

My breath was coming in and out of my chest at an accelerated rate, and each time I breathed in, it felt like I was doing it through a straw. My throat was tight, and I felt like I couldn't catch my breath.

Something clattered to the floor at my feet.

When the hell had I ended up on my knees on the floor?

Judging by the way my legs were tingling as blood flow tried to get to where it needed to go, it'd been a while.

Eyes flicking to the piece of metal that'd fallen, my heart skipped a beat.

It was the pre-cut metal of Verity's father's yet-to-be-forged sword.

The one I'd cut before this whole fucking disaster had started.

I leaned forward, closed my fingers around the cool metal, took a few deep breaths and tried to compose myself.

I still couldn't breathe, but I could focus on this while I tried to pull myself back together.

Getting up, I fired up the forge and shoved the piece of metal into the fire.

After donning my gloves, I picked up my tongs, yanked the metal out of the fire and placed it on the anvil. I picked up my hammer, and proceeded to whack the ever-loving shit out of the metal.

I didn't know how long it was before the sword finally started to take shape, but I'd just put it back into the fire for round ninety-five when I heard someone's knock at my door.

Moving to the flimsy door that separated me from the outside world, I came to a halt when I saw her.

"Yes?" I rasped as I opened the door, voice gruff from disuse.

My eyes were blurry.

My body ached.

My head was a pounding mass of flesh that would likely hate me very much the next time I decided to try to sleep, and to put the icing on the cake, I still couldn't breathe.

Ilsa stared back at me the moment I opened the door, and I couldn't read her face.

"She's asking for you."

The hammer dropped from my hand to the floor, and my body followed it down.

I fell to my knees and stayed there so long that Ilsa placed her hand on top of my sweaty head.

"Hurry," she ordered. "Go take a shower, and let's go see her."

I did as she instructed, and the moment I saw Verity's eyes on mine thirty minutes later, I found the ability to breathe correctly again.

My heart, however, would never be the same.

CHAPTER 25

*I wouldn't do anything for a Klondike Bar, but
I'd do some sketchy shit for a cup of coffee.*

-Text from Truth to Verity

Verity

"You're fucking crazy," I told my husband. "Get the hell out of here so I can get dressed."

"We need to sell one of our houses. Mine is the logical choice."

His was the logical house to put on the market, but I'd grown to love it here.

"Did you give your dad his sword?" Truth asked, ignoring my instructions and lying down on the bed where all of my clothes were laying.

"Yes," I grumbled. "You're on my shirt," I yanked it out from under his head, causing him to curse. "Does this make me look fat?"

Truth, not a stupid man, denied my words.

"No," he said. "You're pregnant…not fat. They're completely different things."

That was true.

Apparently, nobody had shared with him that I was pregnant, or me, for that matter. Though, everyone swore they did.

I was chalking it up to my pain killer-induced haze.

Who knew what Truth's excuse had been.

My lips twitched as I remembered Truth's reaction to finding out what I suspected to be a pregnancy.

***

"Oh, God," Truth dropped to his knees beside me, his hand on my back as he ran his large palm up and down the length of my back. "You're not dying, are you?"

"No," I said.

It came out more like 'Nlooogoooooooarghhhhh,' though as I tried to speak and throw up at the same time.

That was the last time I would ever eat eggs again!

"Then why are you throwing up?" he asked, panicked now.

I gasped.

Then stopped throwing up.

The minute I sat up, I narrowed my eyes at him.

He picked up a piece of toilet paper, wiped my face, and cringed a little before throwing the paper in the toilet and flushing it.

Oh, God. He'd just wiped puke off of my face.

Now that was love.

"We're getting a divorce," I decided right then and there.

His brows furrowed.

"What?" he asked in confusion. "Why the hell would we do that?"

"Because I draw the line at you sitting on the floor next to me, wiping puke off my face," I informed him.

I was being irrational, but I couldn't help it.

"And," I snapped. "I can't have your baby right now. I can't even take a shower by myself!"

I held up my casted arm, waving it in his face.

His face that was currently being overtaken by shock.

His face was pale, and his beard was quivering as he tried to figure out how to speak.

"Say something," I snapped at him.

He ran a hand down his face, stopping to tug lightly on his beard, before he cleared his throat.

"I...good?"

"Good?"

"Yeah, good."

I blinked.

"That's it?"

He licked his lips.

"What's it?" He fell backwards onto his ass, and let his large back rest against the bathroom cabinets.

"That's all the reaction I'm going to get?" I asked him. "I told you I'm carrying the heir to your throne!"

"The heir to my throne?"

"Yes!" I snapped.

He held his hands up in defense.

"I'm fucking happy!" he said. "Though, I gotta admit, I'm scared as fuck. We could really fuck some kids up."

That was true. We could.

"Yeah," I agreed. "We could."

We sat in silence for a few long moments.

Then Truth opened his arms, and I dove into them.

"We won't fuck them up," he promised.

"Okay," I said.

I hoped that my voice was more confident than what I was really feeling.

He squeezed me tight.

"I love you."

I buried my face into his neck, and I felt him harden underneath me.

"Is there ever a time when you don't think about sex?" I asked him, a laugh bubbling up my throat.

"Just a minute ago, when that puke and a piece of egg was on your lip, I wasn't thinking about sex."

I smacked him before I got up and brushed my teeth. Then I showed him just how excited I was to be carrying his child.

***

"Are you sure you're okay?" he asked.

He was looking at me, gauging whether I really was okay despite my assurances that I was, and I wanted to strangle him.

I didn't answer him.

He would've stayed, but the mailman rang the doorbell, causing him to sigh and get up.

I tried on the very last thing I had yet to try on, and sighed.

This would have to be good enough, at least until I could admit defeat and go to a fucking maternity store that sold clothes for big girls.

"What is this?" Truth asked from the doorway, startling me.

I looked up, saw the long box, and smiled.

"Open it."

He did and paused at the sight of the bike seat.

"I just thought, you know, since you like the other bike better, that you'll start riding it again if you have a different bike seat," I said softly.

Truth's eyes were shining with happiness.

"Yeah," he said. "And how did you know what kind to get?"

Dare I tell him that I'd just sent his old one to get reupholstered?

When I'd had the conversation over the phone about the bike seat after I'd gotten home from the hospital, the man that'd done the work had spoken to me like I was a complete lunatic.

The leather work that Truth had done himself was phenomenal, and the upholsters hadn't wanted to cover over it. Even after I'd offered him a shitload of money.

What had finally convinced him to do it, though, was the explanation of Destiny and Kenneth, and how they'd done some nasty things on the bike seat, and that my man refused to ride it anymore.

"I asked a few of the boys where they recommended I take it. It was actually Silas, that sexy, older man who gives Big Papa a run for his money…"

"Wait," Truth held up his hand. "You think another man besides me is sexy?"

He tried to reach for me, but I stepped out of his grasp and turned to survey my fourth outfit in the floor to ceiling mirror.

"Yes," I confirmed. "Both men are sexy as hell. Big Papa is sexier, though. Oh man, he is beautiful."

Though, that was only because Silas still scared the shit out of me.

Big Papa was like a sexy, older teddy bear. He was a really good friend who I could talk to about pretty much anything.

"That's just wrong," Truth muttered, holding the bike seat above his head and inspecting it. "This detail work is amazing."

It was.

The upholsterer was amazing, and I was contemplating stealing Truth's other bike seat so I could do it all over again.

"Kind of presumptuous of you, though, to get the back seat done, too."

I grinned.

"Yeah," I said. "But I figured why not."

He snorted and set the seat down on the bed, right on top of my white halter top, and I rolled my eyes.

"Looks good, baby."

I looked down at the seat where he was fingering the lettering.

His seat said 'Mr. Truth' while mine said, 'Mrs. Truth.'

The rest of it was decorated with words. My words to Truth.

I wasn't sure he was going to like them at first. I was convinced that he would be mad that I desecrated his property, but he seemed genuinely happy that I'd done it.

"The bike seat or my outfit?" I teased.

He didn't look up from the seat.

He was still reading the words.

I love you. I love your face. I love the way your beard makes me shiver. I love the pretty words that come out of your mouth when you're trying to make me laugh. One day, we're going to part, and the only thing I want you to remember when I'm no longer of this Earth is that not a day went by that I didn't thank my lucky stars for you.

It was simple. Sweet. And just so happened to also have been our wedding vows.

Something that I'd only figured out after I'd called the chapel for more photos from our wedding. Apparently, at the time, drunk me only thought that one 8x10 would be enough.

It wasn't.

First, because my GG wanted one for her shop and for her house. Also because I wanted one in every single room of our home, something that Truth was still coming to terms with.

Then, with unrushed movements, he placed the bike seat carefully down on the bed, walked over to me, and placed both of his big hands on my face.

Gently, oh so fucking gently, he brought my face to his, and kissed me.

It was sweet.

But, just as suddenly, it wasn't sweet anymore.

Ever since I'd almost died, everything Truth did was with every bit of effort he could muster.

His kisses were deeper. His hugs were just a little bit longer, a little bit tighter. The sex…well I couldn't complain there. Everything was more intense, the feelings, the way he held me afterward.

So yeah, me almost getting killed twice in one day was bad, but I couldn't say I was completely dissatisfied with the after-effects.

Unfortunately, I could tell that Truth was still haunted about it, though.

But right now, with his lips on mine, his hand snaking down to part my folds, he didn't seem haunted at all.

In fact, he seemed focused on his goal.

His goal being my orgasm.

Something he accomplished seconds later as he dipped his fingers into the back of my pants, and thrust two fingers deep into my pussy.

"Ohhh," I breathed.

My eyes closed as he started to suck on my neck, coaxing my orgasm to the surface.

I arched, rubbing my aching nipples against his chest.

The rasp of my lace bra dragging along the hard plane of his chest had a moan leeching out of my throat.

My eyes crossed, and I yanked his beard down, bringing the rest of his face with it, and slammed my lips against his own.

"Fuck," he growled against my lips. "You want me, baby?"

Of course I wanted him. What kind of a stupid question was that?

I nodded anyway, though, just in case he needed the encouragement.

He grinned his Cheshire cat grin, showing me his teeth, and then reared up off of me—all the while being careful of my belly as he moved.

Our clothes were discarded. The bed was raked clean of the rest of my clothing, which likely were going to need to be vacuumed or lint rolled from all of the cat hair.

Then he was maneuvering me onto my side, and crawling into the bed behind me.

He brought his hand to the back of my thigh and lifted it, scooting even closer and allowing his hardened cock to drag deliciously through the lips of my sex.

I bit my lip, my head going back, and moaned—long and loud.

I reached down between my legs and captured his hard cock, squeezing the tip lightly as I lined him up with my entrance.

The moment he felt himself positioned, he gave a loud grunt and thrust inside of me.

He didn't fit.

At least not yet, anyway.

So he had to play with my clit, coaxing my body to produce more wetness to ease his way inside.

Luckily, he didn't have to do much more than look pretty, because the moment his rough fingers found my clit, I started to be pulled under.

At first I was able to think.

But it quickly became apparent that there would be no thinking when Truth's cock was inside of me, so I gave up and just focused on how good it felt.

I loved the way his hard cock filled me up when he thrust forward and even how it left me feeling bereft as he pulled away.

I looped my hand up, tangling it in his hair, and started to move my hips as best as I could despite him holding me exactly where he wanted me.

"Baby?"

I ignored him, and he moved his large hand down between my thighs and went back to playing with my clit.

"You okay?" he rasped against my ear.

I bit my lip.

I was so fucking close, and all he wanted to do was fucking talk to me.

"Perfect," I gasped. "Fuckin' hurry!"

He growled, leaned down, and drug his bearded jaw along the length of my shoulder that he could reach without moving.

And I had to say, the man was a freakin' genius. The faster and harder he thrust, the more I wanted to scream out with pleasure.

But, alas, I couldn't. Not and walk out of the bedroom with my head held high.

Though, I guess, technically, Ghost wasn't in a great mood lately, anyway. Hearing Truth and I have sex was the least of his worries.

Seanshine, though, would happily make my husband feel bad for forgetting about them.

Me, though, I didn't care. One second I was contemplating the men outside, and the next Truth rolled me over onto my knees, holding onto my hips until I could get my knees and arms underneath of me.

Once I was up and not squishing our baby, he returned to fucking me. This time it was rougher. Less sweet and more raw.

Thrust, thrust.

Smack.

I gasped, my eyes springing open, and turned my head to glare at him over my shoulder.

"Fuck, Truth!" I gasped. "What the fuck?"

My words, however, were lost on him as he picked up his pace.

Our bodies were smacking together, echoing off the empty walls of our shared bedroom.

"Come," he ordered. "Use your fingers if you have to."

I didn't need to.

He didn't even need to tell me to come, because I was halfway gone before he'd even finished his sentence.

I cried out and clamped down on his cock, my face burying in the pillow that was half under my body, half under my head.

He cursed and bucked wildly as his thrusts became erratic and uneven.

Then I heard his groan of completion as he followed me over the edge into the abyss.

"Fucking better and better every single time," Truth said, letting his sweaty body lean over my naked back. "I love you, Very."

I smiled.

"I love you, too, Truth."

His growl of happiness was made against the back of my neck, and I shivered as the words hit home.

I loved this man. I loved the way he left me for hours on end, and I'd find him building a sword, all hot and sweaty into the wee hours of the night. I loved the way his eyes lit up when I brought him tea, juice, or coke for no reason. I loved the way he would curl me close when he felt I'd gotten too far away from him during the night or even while we were eating dinner.

But, most of all, I loved how he loved me. Without limits.

He didn't care that anyone thought he was whipped or too attentive to me. He only cared about what he and I thought, and that was everything.

***

Two hours and a sated vagina later, I was trying not to fall asleep as I waited for dinner to be ready.

We were all gathered around the bar eating when something popped.

The food on the stove. Hot grease that Big Papa was using to fry some chicken. The problem was that there were a lot of people eating, and he had a lot of it to do.

Aaron and his wife, Imogen. Tommy Tom and his wife, Tally, as well as their daughter who was putting the chicken away just about as fast as Big Papa could fry it. Then there was me and Truth. Seanshine and his most current date—who happened to be Tommy Tom's sister. The two former prospects who were full blown members of The Dixie Wardens MC now. Their dates. Then Big Papa's date, whom, I might add, was a complete and total bitch.

The pop of the fryer caused me to jump and turn. Food went everywhere, and Ghost, who'd been standing about a foot away holding a plate for Big Papa grunted. Then he was moving, turning and twisting at the same time he yanked his t-shirt off over his head.

I saw that the plate of chicken was on the table, saved by Ghost before he'd yanked his t-shirt off.

The split-second I saw of the back of his t-shirt before it was on the ground showed oil streaking his back, and dripping down his pants.

"Oh, shit!" I gasped, coming to my feet as did a few of the other ladies that were sitting surrounding the table.

Three pregnant ladies, all waiting for food, didn't make for patient waiting.

"Ghost!" Tally gasped, already moving around the table.

I made it around the other way just as Imogen got off her stool, both of us jumping over Tank who looked annoyed that we would dare disturb his sleep.

That was how three pregnant ladies, all hormonal as hell, were found standing around a practically naked man who was in the process of taking off his pants when their men came in to see what the commotion was all about.

"Imogen!" Aaron barked. "Step away from the fryer!"

Imogen obeyed, but only far enough that she could bend to pick up Ghost's gun that had fallen to the floor in his haste to get his pants off.

I squatted down and gathered his pants, as well as the phone that'd been in his hand.

A text message was on the screen, and I couldn't help myself.

Ghost (8:30 PM): Don't let my wife do it. I'll come get her.

Silas (8:34 PM): You can't come get her, you're dead.

Ghost (8:35 PM): Not anymore.

I hastily placed the items on the counter, and then turned back to the man who was the center of attention.

And almost blanched.

He had burns.

Oh, God did he have burns. They were everywhere. All over his body. They even distended down into his boxer briefs, disappearing from view.

Holy. Shit.

"Ghost," I breathed. "Are you okay?"

I was breathless for a few reasons.

One, Ghost had just been burned, possibly badly.

Two, Ghost was practically naked, and despite his burns, he looked good.

Three, Ghost had a wife, and he was about to go get her.

Oh, shit.

"Jesus Christ, man," Sean said as he pushed in between us. "You're going to need someone to look at this."

"No."

Simple. Direct. That was our Ghost.

"Sorry, darlin'," Big Papa's date, Terril, sauntered up, placing her hands on Ghost's back. "But I agree with him."

"Don't. Touch. Me."

The words, although low in pitch, felt like a scream in the busy, chaotic room.

Every man, woman, and child felt those nearly whispered words deep down to their souls.

"Sorry, hon," Terril backed away with her hands raised.

I bit my lip and turned to find Truth, who made big eyes at me and gestured at me with his hand.

I left the commotion of the kitchen and walked into my man's arms.

"What's with that look on your face," he asked, tilting his head down to study my eyes.

His hand had gone to my distended belly, absently running his big, rough palm down over the top of it.

The baby, the booger who only kicked for his father, nudged his hand, causing Truth to smile.

I moved until my mouth hovered just over Truth's ear, though he did have to bend down a little to allow me to do it.

"I saw Ghost's phone. He dropped it while all that happened," I gestured with my hand to the spectacle over my shoulder.

Now Sean's date, Ellen, who I'd seen looking at Jessie James more tonight than Sean, walked into the room, took one look at the man who was trying to disentangle himself from the melee of people that were making a fuss over him, and turned around and fled.

Jessie James (I still don't know why the hell I called him his entire name, but I wasn't the only one), followed after her with one look at Sean to make sure he wasn't paying attention.

I winced inwardly. That was going to be a mess if it ever went past the innocent stage I could tell it was at right now.

"And?" Truth asked, oblivious to the soap opera going on around him.

"And on his phone, it said that he was going to get back his wife," I whispered just as quietly as before.

He blinked.

Then a broad grin broke out over his face.

"Fuck yeah."

EPILOGUE

*When confronting a woman, you should always
make sure her man isn't around the corner.*

-Fact of Life

Verity

7 months later

Verity (9:34 A.M.): That's it. I'm selling this kid on eBay.

Truth (9:39 A.M.): What'd he do now?

*Verity (9:40 A.M.): He shit on my shirt. And my pants. I'm pretty
sure I have it in my hair.*

Truth (9:54 A.M.): Take a shower and wash your clothes.

Verity (10:03 A.M.): He shit on your latest sword, too.

*Truth (10:31 A.M.): Don't be silly. You made him. You should sell
him on Etsy.*

I burst into peals of laughter, rolling over onto my stomach as I
did.

The man I loved was a funny one, I'd give him that.

A cry of anger and pissed off 'you woke me up laughing' came
from the baby's playpen that was set up in the corner of my office,
and I sighed.

I should've known better, but it wasn't my fault.

It was all Truth's fault. Every last, single bit of it.

"Do you have a minute?"

I looked up to find the manager, Brian Staganoff, standing in the doorway of my open office.

"Sure," I said carefully. "What's up?"

I was about to fire him. In fact, I'd planned on doing that after lunch when Truth had time to come and get his son.

And yes, I say his son, because he definitely wasn't my son. There was no evidence beside him coming out of my vagina…and even then I could play that off due to me being delirious and high on the good medications.

"I need to apologize for my behavior a few nights ago."

My brows went up.

"Oh, yeah?" I asked, leaning back in my chair.

This should be good.

Hearing him explain why he called another waitress a cunt in front of the entire fucking bar should entertain me greatly. And yes, I did say another waitress.

Apparently, he'd done it before, quite a few times. This had been the only time I'd been present to hear it.

"Yes, Ma'am," he said through clenched teeth.

He really, really didn't want to be here apologizing to me.

In fact, he likely wouldn't have bothered had my husband not been present as well.

I'd been willing to give him the benefit of the doubt, at first, but after getting the fourth complaint about his behavior and deplorable attitude today, I knew that something else had to give.

He had to go.

Though, I was willing to admit I hated firing people, even if they were douche canoes like this one.

"Okay," I said, ready to hear him explain why in the world he thought it was okay to tell a woman that the only thing she was good for was her warm cunt.

Though, that had been after he'd called her an actual cunt.

I listened to him apologize, and barely contained the laughter in my eyes when Truth showed up a few minutes into his explanation and subsequent apology. He listened, rolled his eyes, and made jacking off motions when the sweetness of Brian's voice made both of us wince.

"I'm sorry, Brian," I said. "I was going to do this later, after lunch, but since you're already in here and you know what this is about, I'm going to have to let you go. I can't have any employees working at this pub who don't respect the patrons and their coworkers. Truth's grandfather cared for his waitresses, and he would never be okay with the way you treated Bonita two nights ago."

Brian's entire body locked. "You can't fire me."

My brows rose, and Truth started to vibrate with laughter as he tried to keep it quiet and not alert the man that he was standing behind him.

"Yes," I pushed back from my chair and stood up. My pants, which had been digging into my belly, finally loosened, allowing me to breathe again. I'd gained a ton of weight (over seventy pounds) during my pregnancy, and still, months after having our son, I was trying to lose the weight. Slowly but surely. In the meantime, all of my clothes still fit like shit, and my pants were tight as hell and digging into my belly when I sat down for longer than three seconds. "I can. I'm sorry to have to do this, and I hate that I have to do it, but as of now, you no longer are employed by Breaker Pub."

"You're a fucking bitch," he said, ripping off his name tag and tossing it.

The problem was that he tossed it in the direction of our son, who I could hear moving around in the pack and play.

The moment the name badge hit the wall beside his head, Ernest Junior, better known as EJ, started to really scream.

I closed my eyes for the next bit.

That was because I had shit in my hair. I had shit on my shirt and pants. I also had vomit down my back that I was trying really hard not to overthink. And Truth, being the overprotective man he was over his wife and child, struck.

He grabbed Brian by the coat collar, yanked him to face him, and then decked him.

"Mother. Fucker."

***

Four hours later, I was fairly sure that I'd talked Brian out of pressing charges.

Though, to do that I had to offer him a severance check that was quite substantial.

And did Truth care one single bit that he'd cost the pub over four thousand dollars? Hell no.

He was sitting there, EJ in his arms, staring at the game on the TV with Sean sitting next to him.

A recently broken up Sean, who was less Seanshine and more Seanstorm.

Though, I didn't call him that to his face.

"Would you stop pacing?" Truth growled without breaking away from the stupid fucking game that he was watching.

I narrowed my eyes.

"The quarterback gets hurt, and they lose the game in the fifth."

Truth froze, then calmly leaned over, handed EJ to Sean who was trying not to laugh, and stood up.

Carefully, he turned around, rounded the couch, and then started in my direction.

Me, being me, never knew when to shut up.

Had I known, I wouldn't have continued to bait him.

"And they also lose a wide receiver because he tore his ACL. They lost in overtime," I sneered at him.

Truth didn't even stop.

He bent low once he reached me, snaked his arm around the backs of my thighs, and stood.

"Ommph," I grunted, trying to push up.

Truth wouldn't allow it. The moment I started to push against his shoulders to alleviate the pressure on my belly, he smacked me on the ass. Hard.

I shrieked.

Sean grinned at me the entire way into our shared bedroom, and right before the door slammed on his laughing face, I flipped him off. Because I was mature and shit like that.

Sean's laughter was shut off the moment the door slammed shut, and I gasped because I was then flying through the air and landing on the bed.

The moment my back hit the comforter, I gasped and started to roll away.

Truth followed me down, though, refusing to let me move away from him.

"You wanted my attention, baby," he growled, getting so close to my face that his beard tickled my chin. "And you have it."

I gasped, instinctively opening my thighs to the man, and licked my lips when Truth's hard cock immediately ground into me.

I was wearing a pair of leggings which seemed to be the only thing that fit my ass and belly well enough for me to wear them for long periods of time without wanting to slice my belly fat off with a paper cutter.

The look in Truth's eyes, the one that showed me that I was sexy no matter what I looked at, was my undoing, though.

"I'm mad," I said breathlessly.

He grinned, his mouth dropping down to my lips.

"I can tell," he said. "What are you mad about?"

His hand was on the move, starting at my side and moving down until he was at the top of my leggings, his hand delving under my shirt.

I sucked my belly in when he plunged his hand inside my pants and widened my legs, allowing him complete access.

He grinned as he pulled away from me, watching my eyes as he let his fingers play along the folds of my sex.

"I'm mad," I swallowed thickly, trying to concentrate. It was nearly impossible with the way his finger was circling my clit, though. "Because you just cost us four grand."

"Four grand well spent," he said, bending down to bite my nipple through the tunic I was wearing.

I squeezed my eyes shut and moaned.

"I…I…"

"You what?" he rasped.

I couldn't think.

"It was uncalled for," I told him bluntly, trying to gather my thoughts and finding myself unable to.

He growled against my breast, causing my entire body to tingle. Then he was up and moving, yanking my leggings down just far enough to expose my ass.

Then he started working on his belt—which didn't take too long.

Thank God.

And when he was plunging that hard cock inside of me, pressing my legs forward to my chest, I really didn't care about much of anything any longer.

"It was totally called for," he told me as he buried himself inside of me. "Any time I feel that you or my son are being disrespected, you can expect the same results."

Then he pulled out and thrust back inside. Hard. And I lost all ability to care about anything else but him.

That's, of course, when the baby started to cry from the living room, and I started to laugh. EJ reminded me that there were other people in the house other than us.

"He's going to be pissed," I informed him breathily. "If I don't come get him and feed him ASAP."

I'd found that EJ was a whole lot like me, in that when he wanted to be fed, it'd better happen on his time schedule or I'd regret it.

Truth grunted, not stopping.

I ran my hands up his sides, causing him to shiver. Then his eyes moved to mine.

Seconds later, he started to come, and I watched him give me everything he had to give.

My eyes fell closed, and I gasped, trying to catch my breath.

Something that was much easier when Truth's heavy weight removed itself from my body.

"Stay," Truth murmured as he got up. "I'll go get him."

I rolled onto my belly, feeling the hardness in my breasts that signaled a feeding was imminent.

I got up anyway. I had to go clean myself up.

EJ was a grazer. He took his time eating, and since we had a party to go to tonight at the club, I didn't have time to waste.

Not to mention that I'd just had sex with my man and had to clean up before I held my kid. That was just gross.

I hurried to the bathroom, grabbing a towel off the rack above the toilet. My eyes caught on the decorative metal, and I smiled. That'd been the newest addition to Truth's effort to fix up my old home.

And I had to admit, over the last seven months that he'd really been working on it, it looked a zillion times better.

"You gonna sit there all day with that towel between your legs, or are you going to feed my son?"

I tossed Truth a glare, wiped myself while he watched, and tossed the dirty towel into the hamper beside the door.

"He's not crying right now," I pointed out.

Truth turned.

"He's sucking on my neck. I'd say that he is hungry, whether he's crying or not."

I sighed and reached for a new nursing tank that was hanging on the back of the door. Once in place, I reached for a pair of panties, slipped both feet into them, and settled them on over my hips.

"Give him," I ordered. "And go get in the shower. We have to leave in half an hour."

Truth handed him over, but chose to watch as I settled down in our bed and deftly situated pillows around my body for support.

"You have that down to an art," Truth observed.

I did. That was what happened when you had a child chained to your breast for half the day.

I pulled my shirt down, and moved EJ so that he was in a comfortable position with his head resting on the pillow.

Before I could offer my breast to EJ, though, Truth did the honors for me, and I raised a brow at him.

"Such a turn on," he murmured, running his hand down EJ's cheek. "Watching you care for our son feels like a dream come true."

Happiness filled my heart.

"I like watching you with him, too. It makes me feel warm and gooey inside."

Truth grinned.

"Feed our son. I'll go get Sean up and off the couch. Get him to help load the car. Anything else you need us to do besides take the groceries off the table?" he inquired.

I shook my head, then felt my heart leap when he dropped his mouth to mine.

"Verity?"

"Yes?" I breathed against his mouth.

"I love you."

Tears filled my eyes.

I was an emotional mess.

"I love you, too."

With one last kiss on the lips, he was gone, and I was left alone with my child, thanking the Lord that I got drunk in Vegas.

***

Ghost

I flipped the liter open and closed.

Open.

Closed.

Open.

Closed.

A cat hissed.

I threw the liter at it, and the cat hissed again, this time directly at me.

Fucking cat.

"Here, kitty kitty!"

I looked up to see her pushing the screen door open, and my heart started to pound.

"What's that?"

I froze when she started walking toward me, unaware that I was deep in the shadows less than five feet in front of her.

Her breath hitched when she bent to pick up the liter, and a small moan fell from her perfect, bowtie lips.

"No."

ABOUT THE AUTHOR

Lani Lynn Vale is married to the love of her life that she met in high school. She fell in love with him because he was wearing baseball pants. Ten years later they have three perfectly crazy children and a cat named Demon who likes to wake her up at ungodly times in the night. They live in the greatest state in the world, Texas. She writes contemporary and romantic suspense, and has a love for all things romance. You can find Lani in front of her computer writing away in her fictional characters' world...that is until her husband and kids demand sustenance in the form of food and drink.

Made in the USA
Middletown, DE
19 October 2023